Hoisted

Petard

Lyle Michaelson

Table of Contents

Dedication

This story was written with aspirations to increase awareness.

Acknowledgments

Nathan and Parker, thank you so much for your unrelenting support, insight and love. This book was not possible without both of you in my corner.

About the Author

Lyle Michaelson lives in the Pacific Northwest with his wife, Sarah, and son, Myles. He is a clinical social worker who has worked in the mental health field for two decades in a variety of roles, currently as a therapist and consultant.

Part I: The Onset of Psychosis

Chapter One

I never felt like I knew myself very well. I was just some dude, smart enough, sometimes clever. Sometimes dumb, even a lush. I tried to play sports, get girls and all that kind of shit, with limited success. But that's not what this story is about. It is about the journey I went on after losing control of my mind. It suddenly began playing tricks on me and blew up in my face. But, I don't want you to feel sorry for me. Let's be clear about one thing: this is not a sad story.

Strange maybe. But not sad.

It all started when I was sitting in a lecture hall at the University of Washington. It was the beginning of my sophomore year of college, and I started hearing voices for the first time that day and didn't have a clue what was happening. I stood up in the middle of a crowded lecture and hollered in distress. I didn't say any words, just a visceral reaction, "Whoa!"

This was my inaugural hallucination that was not caused by recreational drug use of any kind. What I experienced in the lecture hall that day was different from any previous high, or low for that matter. It sounded like a group of people were softly singing behind the hallway door ten feet to my left. That's how the whispers began for me. They just started. All of a sudden, I could hear them, and no one else could. I scanned the room, looking for the source of the whispers in my head. *Are there speakers? Why isn't anyone else reacting? Did I miss something?*

"Shhh. Hush," the whispering voices sang. They were singing a gentle song at first, gradually becoming threatening like a group of people shushing in unison. I began to verbally respond to the voices in the middle of class like a performance artist at a regional sketch theater. Somehow the whispering voices communicated that a giant tidal wave was about to crash through the lecture hall and wash everyone away. It doesn't make sense now, but in that moment, I felt compelled to warn the students sitting around me.

"Get out!" I hollered with all of the energy in my body, my voice echoing off the rafters awkwardly as everyone else sat silently watching the show.

My outburst was delivered with such authenticity that I convinced some of my classmates something dangerous was happening. People began to stand up and look around, searching for the cause of my distress. I scanned the room, looking for the tidal wave to come bursting through one of the giant windows. Students stared back at me with confusion. Then, after a few minutes, laughter erupted among some of my classmates and wafted over the bellowing voices in my head. I sat back down and tried to compose myself, but it was too late.

This was the initial onset of schizophrenia, in clinical terms.

That's how it started. Nothing up to that point in my life gave me any sort of indication. All of a sudden, I was crazy, experiencing a variety of auditory hallucinations. Mostly the voices sounded like soft whispers, but they could also become angry and loud. I felt something was wrong with me.

As the rest of the class sat in total confusion, I disconnected from them and engaged with the voices in my head, trying to understand them. They were no longer screaming about a tidal wave. They had morphed back into a sort of whisper from the heavens, momentarily pleasant. Imagine a very nice surround sound system, softly projecting the voices of men and women whispering.

I don't know how long I was sitting there before the security guards arrived. But soon, I was being dragged forcefully from the room. My shoes fell off on the way out. This was the type of scene a person can't take their eyes off of. A slow-moving train wreck. Most of America doesn't know what to think about people who hear voices or even know how to spell schizophrenia. I was held face down by University security guards on the tile outside the lecture hall. It didn't take long for the university police to show. My introduction to the world of mental illness was met with violent force. I was treated like a criminal. Hauled off to jail

4

like a crook. I ended up in a holding cell at the university police department. They didn't even book me into jail, thinking I was just another wannabe frat boy who got too fucked up on something and tweaked out in class.

The officers at the station gave me my first experience with law enforcement and mental illness. The treatment is similar to how a grown man would treat his dog in a moment of discipline. I was utterly distracted by the voices, mumbling nonsensically back to them. My eyes were fixated on the wall in front of me with a 1,000-mile stare like a crazy person. And that's how the cops treated me. But what else are the cops supposed to do? Reason with me? I could not communicate at that moment because I was too psychotic. The truth is, I don't really blame folks for the poor treatment. This kind of brain disorder is bizarre enough that most people aren't comfortable communicating with a person responding to voices. A soft sense of humor can be the most useful approach. As it turns out, the law enforcement field does not attract many comics.

"Are you on drugs or mentally ill?" A simple, direct question. So simple that it's condescending. So direct it's offensive to the bleeding hearts out there. Tiny violin, right? City cops with a certain amount of experience generally tend to break social issues down to the simplest terms possible. I didn't know the answer to the question. My adrenaline rush began to subside, and I became oriented to the situation. The directness of the inquiry provided feedback necessary for me to realize my behavior was being perceived as dysfunctional. So maybe cops aren't assholes, after all, I don't know. I could tell that the officer had my best interests in mind. He was not offering to hug me or provide emotional support, but he wanted to know who to call for assistance: mental health services or drunk tank/drug services. I appreciate that he gave a shit either way.

The officer acquired enough information to call a mental health professional instead of just letting me sit in the cell to see if I came down from something. After the person arrived to assess me, I refused to answer their questions. Which was too bad because I really *should* have been forced to stay in a psych ward for a few days. Getting evaluated by a psychiatrist and getting on some meds would have been beneficial. But, I was not a danger to myself or anyone else, so they couldn't hold me against my will. And although I was uncomfortable with the whispering voices, they weren't telling me to hurt anyone. I only wanted to get the fuck out of there. This being the case, under state law and given the mental health resources at hand, I wasn't going to be placed into a mental health bed. I didn't commit a crime, I was just a lunatic. I had an ID card from UW in my wallet, so the cops knew I was a student. They phoned the university, who, in turn, contacted my parents.

So there I was, locked in a cage, listening to these brand new whispering voices in my head. I was desperate to understand what they wanted from me. I tried to focus and understand them. I could pick up a few words here and there, but nothing enough to track. Although I couldn't understand what they were saying, the voices made me feel like I had a responsibility to decipher their message. To glean some kind of purpose from their presence. The passing of time was very different while I was under the spell of these voices, non-linear and just sort of fluid in all directions. Suddenly, my parents were in front of my jail cell, desperate to know what was wrong with me and how they could help.

"Honey, what's happening?" I was in a psychotic state, but the distress in my mother's eye was obvious. Schizophrenics have an equal emotional intelligence to the general population, perhaps even better. The jumbled group of words and sounds that I verbally responded to my mother with at that point, from a jail cell, was absurd. No logic, didn't make any sense. Of course, I can't recall what I said, but my mother wasn't speaking to her son per se. She was speaking to a new version of her son. A mentally ill version, for the first time. This aspect is a shocking part of the illness. It can affect people who've been nurtured and cared for with great love and skill. It's not man-made. Rather, a chemical imbalance in the brain. It is common for family members to search for a reason to point at. A source. Something to attribute the onset of the illness to. My mother began to search. Frantically calling hotlines, family members in search of a solution to this problem. Is there a useful explanation for why her son, who led a stable life for almost twenty years, went nuts? Professionals were consulted, and an appointment with an outpatient psychiatrist was made urgently.

My mom coaxed me into their car, and my father drove us toward the Wenatchee home I grew up in. I was able to stay silent for the entire 3-hour drive. I slept in brief intervals, but little rest was attained. I had been through an experience so foreign, so bizarre and intense that my eyes felt like they were bugging out of my skull. I could feel the throbbing of my pulse radiating on my pupils as blood was pooling around the front of my brain. My body knew something had changed, something was wrong with my brain, and it was directing more blood flow to the area in an effort to heal.

Soon enough, we were back home, and my mother encouraged me to get some rest. I complied, walked inside like a good boy, went to my room, and laid down, humiliated. I was confused about how I ended up here. I had a strong desire to leave. I felt the need to get out, flee. Where would I go? Back to my apartment in Seattle, I supposed. Obviously, I wasn't in contact with any peers at the time. My cell phone was confiscated by my father, who was thumbing through it to access any information. I was isolated. I felt insulted as I lay in bed. Thinking about the way I had been treated. The way I had been physically forced out of class and shoved into a jail cell quickly turned my resentment into anger and contributed to my desire to leave, to run. But I hadn't built up the courage yet, so I just laid there, chasing my thoughts.

Helpless and paranoid, I unsuccessfully attempted to masturbate in an effort to activate a single endorphin in my brain that could provide even a second of satisfaction. But my thoughts were pulling me in every direction as the voices continued to communicate with me. A gentle knock interrupted my distress, "Jack, do you want some casserole?" My first meal as an individual living with mental illness had arrived. I decided to break bread with the voices in my head.

"Of course I do. Bring it in, please. I don't want to talk right now." This was the first coherent interaction with a human since the voices started in the lecture hall. My mother treated me similarly to a mental patient at a facility. She delivered the meal with a clinical delicateness. I could see she was being cautious with me, not wanting to cause me to react, which really hurt. She was treating me as if I were not the person she raised, like I was a stranger.

Chapter Two

People living with schizophrenia experience the illness in entirely unique ways. But, for a person to have the illness, they must experience some kind of sensory stimulation that no one else does. It could be a visual hallucination, a smell, a physical feeling, or hearing something that does not exist. I'm not talking about eating mushrooms and hallucinating either. Something like that can't be caused by drugs. Many people hallucinate after ingesting different types of mind-altering drugs, then stop, and the hallucinations eventually disappear. In order to be schizophrenic, it must be organic. It's a biological disorder of the brain. The human brain is the most complex phenomenon in the world, and we don't understand everything about how this illness occurs. No machine can be hooked up to a person or put on like a helmet to measure the person's degree of illness or symptoms. We only have the observation of human behavior to guide our understanding of schizophrenia. Don't get me wrong, pharmaceutical companies have certainly made a lot of strides in terms of producing medications that mitigate the symptoms of schizophrenia in ways that allow the person to function at a much higher level. But, no one can fully understand how any individual experiences the illness. And at this point in my life, people were trying to figure out how they could help with my unique experience of this disorder. So, my folks lined up a bunch of appointments to that end.

I saw different outpatient psychiatrists over the next two weeks, almost daily. I told the shrinks about a night of ecstasy use I had two days before the voices started whispering in my head. The shrinks were unwilling to prescribe any antipsychotic meds until three weeks after the ecstasy use. Exhausted and defeated, my parents tried to enlist the help of close family members. I was physically wrestled down by my brother-in-law several times over the coming weeks after becoming belligerent. Which I don't blame him for at all. He was trying to help, and he did. I was clearly ill. I put them through the wringer. They were trying to protect me from myself, and they did. I am privileged in this way and many others. I could have easily been camping out in an alternative stratosphere, with no one to protect me from the influence of the voices.

As the struggle to find help for me continued, my desire to run away grew. The illness influenced me to distance myself from my family. The resentment and anger festered underneath the surface of my skin as the voices continued whispering messages into my consciousness. The Columbia River was nearby, and the whispers started pushing me toward it, "Move the water," they whispered. I thought God was speaking to me. It was a similar sort of delusion to the tidal wave I expected to wash away my class at the university lecture hall.

My shell was growing thicker. The wall between my perception and reality was expanding. In my mind, I was being held captive. A prisoner in a cage. The whispers were very distressing. I was scared. They started to sound like screeches and gasps echoing inside my skull, like a dark concrete room full of ghosts. I responded to the voices with fear. I shouted at them, asked them to leave. Subsequently, I found myself locked in my childhood bedroom with my 220-pound brother-in-law pinning the door shut. I had lived in this room during my formative years. Now, at age nineteen, I was being there held against my will, and my mind had abandoned me. I sat on my bed staring at the bedroom door. I'd worried about so many things laying in this bed growing up, but had never thought to be afraid of my own mind. I was not living in reality.

The days crept by like a bad dream. There were moments of clarity as I began work on coping with the whispering voices and came to grips with the fact that I was the only person hearing them. I was starting to adapt to the illness a bit, to work around the voices. I was able to pull my focus together for fleeting moments, ignore the whispers, and have brief conversations with family members. I was improving. My perception waned toward reality as the whispers in my head quieted for a couple days. They would come in waves, then quiet down for a while. The crackerjack security detail around me was beginning to back off.

As I started to find ways to distract myself from the voices, they began to grow louder and more powerful again. They began whispering messages of danger, "The water is coming." I didn't feel this was necessarily a danger to me. Rather, the community was in danger. I was the chosen recipient of the message for some reason. The voices became clearer, and I understood their words and sentences. A heavy feeling of responsibility fell over me.

The messages came in waves. I could understand the whispers stating "Water" with a concerned tone. Water? What the fuck does that mean? Somehow, and I'm not sure how this occurred, the idea of water morphed into paranoia that the area was about to be soaked by the most significant rain since Noah's Ark. The nearby Columbia River was going to become a giant sea, my parents' home and the entire community was about to be underwater. The stress I began to feel was completely irrational, of course.

Nevertheless, it was distressing, and I was contemplating how I could save the great people of the Wenatchee Valley from these impending biblical rains. The urgency of the message was severe. I needed to take action on behalf of humanity. So, I played possum. I went along with the synthetic normalcy within the home and waited in isolation for the right time to slip out of the house without being noticed. This is it. Tonight I will make my move.

Chapter Three

As the evening arrived, I complied with all of the directives I received like a good mental patient. After dinner, I went back to my room. The voices were growing more convincing, and I had decided it was time to make my escape. Opening up the window and slipping out into the night seems simple enough. But the psychotic spell I was under made it feel like I was escaping from a high-security prison. I sat awake in the room until I was convinced that my folks were out cold and finally just hopped right out of the window into the backyard and scurried away like a mischievous rat escaping into the darkness. As I took a moment to be present with my freedom, the voices rushed back into my consciousness.

"Water, find the water!" they were screaming. The urgency was deafening.

I matriculated toward the Columbia River like a contributory creek, navigating through orchards and properties. I was convinced that the river required my assistance. The area is covered with apple and cherry orchards, lining the river like a beautiful landscape painting. I waddled down the valley toward the river through orchards and properties.

Hours passed. Due to my disorganized state, I was mainly walking in circles, too distracted to focus. I had lost my way a number of times before looking up to see which direction the river was, then adjusting my path over and over. The sun was now coming up, and I knew that I needed to arrive at my destination before someone spotted me. I had enough self-awareness to know that my behavior would appear bizarre and perhaps even disturbing to most people. But due to my poor directional abilities, I had aimlessly wandered into a residential neighborhood and right into a backyard where I encountered an early-riser enjoying the sunrise with a cup of coffee on her backyard deck. A retiree, most likely, startled to see a disheveled young man wander onto her property first thing in the morning.

"Can I help you, sir?" she asked.

"Yes, ma'am, I really need a shovel badly. We are having a flooding problem, maybe a broken pipe."

Since beginning to hear voices, this was the highest level of manipulation I had engaged in. I made up this lie on the spot. Delusional, I wanted the shovel so that I could dig out a canal to relieve the river of stress and divert water away from homes. The voices inside my head were telling me to do this. Surprisingly the woman handed over a shovel, probably just wanted to get rid of me, and it worked. My journey continued with a shovel propped over my shoulder. It was November in Central Washington. So, it was crispy out. I wasn't totally equipped for the weather wearing sneakers, sweatpants, and a hoodie. However, this was not my concern. I needed to get to work on addressing the impending flood that my internal voices had alerted me to.

The river is a few short miles from my parents' house, but it probably took me ten miles of hiking to find my way there as I would get off track, try to correct, and end up doing laps around the same orchards. But finally, I arrived and bunkered down in a location with thick tree cover, just a stone's throw from the water. I was on a steep embankment. Pedestrians on the riverfront trail were only a few hundred yards removed from my psychotic world. They just as well could have been on another planet. As nightfall arrived, I ventured back out and gathered various loose items from yards and properties. Within a few hours, I constructed a nest for myself out of a BBQ cover, lawn chair, and a tarp. I was only two weeks removed from being a typical student at UW. Obviously, my status as a student was not on my mind. I hadn't even thought about the fact that I was not in school. The illness was more than a distraction, it had taken over my life, and many family members had swept away in its wake.

"They will drown. You must divert the floods!" my internal voices began to amplify their message. I heard several voices reiterating that same point. I needed to dig a canal into diverting the water, or people would drown.

Chapter Four

The operation was underway. I had identified the area where the rain would attack. It would come like a giant faucet opening in the sky, dropping an ocean of water out of a gigantic valve. Again, I would like to reiterate that all of this misinformation was being fed to me by my brain, which had recently been hoisted into an alternative world, a world that existed exclusively inside my skull. I stood at the bottom of the river embankment, staring up a steep grade with a natural wrinkle in the hillside. It was a perfect pre-shaped riverbed leading straight into the Columbia. About twenty-five feet wide and a good fifteen feet deep. As if the hillside was a leg that had the femur removed for a river to flow down it. I became focused on this gash in the hillside, believing that my mission was to enlarge it. That somehow, this would prevent catastrophic flooding. My mind was utterly discombobulated. My wiring was shot. I was looking at a hill on the river bed, thinking that the sky was about to open a tsunami. I am shoveling like I'm digging my child out of a landslide. My wrists were burning from fatigue, and my eyesight was inhibited by mud hanging from my brow.

Who knows how long I was shoveling dirt from the riverbank before the sheriff's department finally showed up. I had covered myself in mud on purpose in some sort of twisted exfoliation effort. It got bizarre by the river. I don't remember what the fuck happened after the digging started. My brain was exploding like an electrical box. I became delirious. If the cops hadn't dragged me up the riverbed like an injured deer, I'd be dead. They detained me with a sort of a fishnet because of the danger I posed to myself, others around me, and the community in general. It was quite a scene to get me out of there. The shovel became a weapon at some point, and I was tased, handcuffed. All of this became common knowledge in the small community and embarrassing for my family, of course. Truly a cringeworthy series of events. I had become the local kid from a respectable family who went nuts. It took a few deputies to handle me. I was advocating on behalf of the public good as I spouted off warnings of the impending flood.

"You don't understand! People will die!"

The road to hell is paved with good intentions. I certainly had the good of the community in mind. But of course, I was out of my mind. When I arrived at the local hospital, I was strapped to a gurney, yelling and screaming. Issuing warnings for the staff at the hospital. Advising them to get their children and elders to a safe place. I was handled by firemen due to the volatile nature of my behavior, and they rolled me into the emergency department. A mask was placed over my head to prevent me from spitting at hospital staff.

From their view, I was secured into a safe position at that point. I was given the sedative to calm me down, Haldol. It was administered by a needle right into my buttcheek, orderlies holding me down. Typically, it goes into the thigh/quad area, but I was squirming so aggressively that it went into my buttocks.

I awoke in a psychiatric hospital in Spokane, Washington. How I ended up there is beyond me. Central Washington must have been lacking mental health beds at the time. So, I was sent off to Spokane, three hundred miles away. After getting admitted to the mental hospital, I started taking meds they gave me to quiet the voices in my head. An antipsychotic regimen of medication. Thus began my journey in and out of medication management. It was hard to accept that I was crazy. I wanted to hold out hope that I was ok. That I am 'normal'. A sort of existential crisis that came along with psychosis, causing me to resist treatment out of self-preservation. It would take a long time for me to accept that I was mentally ill. This was just the beginning.

I began to feel perpetually hungover. The meds I was on were not easy for my system to process. I was so groggy, I might as well have just been drunk. The voices were still speaking. However, they were pushed into the background. I could recognize that they were still trying to communicate, but I was sedated enough to not give a fuck. I slept for days.

I would be prompted to wake up by staff fitted for their work uniforms straight out of a Jack Nicholson movie. To wake up was a task. The pharmaceuticals cast a cloud over my head. The voices were pushed away from my consciousness by the medication. But, I was unable to function like a human at all. I was fed like a dog and led around on a metaphorical leash. The agitation that erupted in my soul regarding how I was being treated was enormous. So angry I could spit. A hideous version of myself was presented to the poor folks at that psychiatric hospital.

My parents fought off a strong desire to pull me off the mental ward and bring me back to their home again. But they are smart. They wouldn't put me in a position to fail. As I would have if I returned to their home. No easy way out of this was going to be available, and my folks understood that. They were in this for the long haul. So, everyone began to take the advice of professionals. The new approach was to avoid feeding into my dysfunctional behavior. There were certain instances throughout this journey when I came into contact with a truly helpful person. Most of the staff at the psychiatric hospital were helpful and had good intentions. But, few people can connect to a person who is coming to grips with the fact that they are now dealing with an ongoing, permanent illness.

The nature of the illness was telling me that nothing was wrong with me. If someone would just listen to me, I could explain. I spent a few days shuffling around the ward, mumbling under my breath about how little everyone knew about me. After about a week or so, the antipsychotic meds they gave me had the whispering voices sounding like a slight breeze, and basically, I was free from their torture. I could still hear them, but they weren't so angry or distracting. However, the perpetual hangover would not go away. I felt like a bag of dicks. I was constipated, bloated, and groggy despite getting about fourteen hours of sleep per day.

A staff member sat down next to me in the TV room. He drank coffee like he was hungover. But, he was comfortable with my presence, and I could tell he wasn't trying to manipulate me in any way. He introduced himself like a regular interaction in the real world. His name was Frank, and he wasn't trying to convince me to adjust my behavior or be compliant with any medication. I told him what was going on, gave him my perspective.

"So nobody will listen to you? Is that it? Like everyone is dismissing your perspective?" he asked between sips.

The way he reflected what he was hearing back to me was simple. He actually wanted to know how I felt. He wasn't trying to present himself as some clinical professional with my solution on a treatment plan.

"Yes, of course. I don't belong here. This is not necessary at all," I proclaimed.

"So, how did you end up here?" Frank inquired.

This was a difficult question for me to answer at the time because I hadn't even begun to consider that my memory was littered with hallucinations, fixed delusions. I was in complete denial. In my view, all of this was a huge mistake, and I was only trying to help. I was trying to help when I got dragged out of class by security. I was trying to help when I dug the ditch by the river. If they would just listen to me, I could get back to school and continue trying to get laid by attending raves on ecstasy. Instead, I was about as popular as a turd in a punch bowl in a mental hospital. I complained to anyone within earshot in that mental ward, not just Frank, but he was the only person who would tolerate me.

"I was trying to provide a community service, and I was taken against my will!" Saying that I believed I was providing community service was not a lie. I believed that to be the truth.

"Well, I'm not going to try to convince you that what you're saying isn't true. But if you want to walk through the chain of events to see if we can get a better idea of how you ended up here, let me know," Frank nonchalantly stated as he stood up to go pour another cup of coffee from the shitty pot the patients also drew from.

This was a useful offer. I was not opposed to having such a discussion. He walked away from me, obviously not overly concerned. He seemed to be trying to hit for a certain average with his approach, not expecting to reach every patient on the mental ward. This was a better alternative to the overly-empathetic, dismissively gentle approach that I was getting from the other social workers and nurses. My entitlement is a bit disgusting, complaining about an overly-empathetic approach from nurses I was getting on a psych ward, maybe I'm an asshole. However, it should be known that I felt my intellect was being insulted. I was crazy, not dumb. Not used to people speaking to me from a top-down approach. I don't mean the type of top-down approach an employee experiences on the job. It felt like the ward staff considered me diminished, a subspecies of human. I had difficulty communicating with anyone in that setting. So, you can see why I was attracted to the approach by the gentleman fighting off his hangover, Frank. At least he wasn't dismissive toward me.

The following day I approached Frank, "When can we meet?"

He was not surprised that I approached him at all, or maybe he just didn't give a fuck. Either way, my inquiry was respected. Frank began to posture a bit, "I'll meet with you at 2 pm today but only to listen to you. I won't have any solutions for you. I don't have a magic wand, and if we are going to work together, it needs to be with a purpose."

I was leveraged for the first time since being admitted to the ward. Frank set the terms of our meeting clearly. A grand piece of human progress, leverage, that is. After all, I needed motivation, and in this case, Frank planted a seed in my brain. Very subtle and artfully done. The blind spots, in my perception, were being challenged respectfully. Obviously, I could not recognize that my psychosis had me operating within a false reality. However, I could see that I was locked in a mental ward. Incarcerated. Frank positioned the conversation in a way that would not allow my hallucinations and delusions to attribute this fact to a conspiracy theory.

The meeting started off with an open-ended approach, "So tell me, why are we here?"

"Like what is the purpose of human life?" I wondered if he would take the conversation in an existential direction.

"No, not like what is the meaning of human life. What is the purpose of the two of us meeting today?" Frank would not go off the tracks despite my effort to drag him into my alternate world.

"Of course. I am hoping you can help me."

"Help you with what?"

"Help me get out of here because I shouldn't be here."

"Ok, I would like to help you get out of here. And I don't want you to be here either. I want to help you move on, stabilize your life. I have read through your notes to see what has been documented about how you ended up here. Why were you digging a ditch for three days in a river bed without eating or sleeping?"

I started unpacking the bizarre incident for Frank. How I was informed by a higher power that biblical rains were coming, and a water diversion was needed to save the community. That I had been selected to dig this diversion. And that somehow, I was strong enough to manually dig a ditch that would be capable of defending the community from an overwhelming tsunami, which was going to pour from the sky. All of that.

I walked Frank through the logic of the ditch digging incident. He took advantage of many opportunities to reflect back at me what he was hearing. Giving me opportunities to correct him. He allowed me to feel like he was working to understand me. He built up a good deal of trust from me in a short period of time. Especially considering I had been nothing but offended by all of my human interaction since being detained at the river and sent to this mental ward. I could tell by the direction he took the conversation at times that he wanted to rule out any mind-altering drugs as a factor in my motivation to dig like a Belgian beaver.

"What type of substances had you been using leading up to the incident?"

"I told you I was not high on anything. I hadn't drunk or used any drugs for two weeks." At a certain point, he moved on from the substance-induced hypothesis. He could clearly see that the voices in my head were real. This psychotic break was organic.

"Listen, Jack, from what you are telling me, you were either chosen by God to be a savior and failed to save yourself from being admitted to a mental hospital. Or you have experienced the onset of a psychotic disorder. You began hearing voices along with other symptoms, and you have responded to them."

I left the meeting frustrated that Frank didn't believe me. I can't say that he didn't listen because I was yapping most of the time. We were in there for seventy-five minutes without a pause in the dialogue. I began to trust him because he was the first mental health professional to listen to me. Before Frank, I told the tale to a number of psychiatrists who intended to medicate me. I felt heard by Frank, and it scared me. I began to believe, if just a fleeting thought, that I was crazy and didn't live in reality.

I complied with the treatment at the mental facility for the following twelve days. This did not entail a great deal of effort on my part. I just agreed to take the medication they presented me with each day. Other than that, I stayed to myself. Frank continued to check in with me, and I knew that he had my best interests in mind. I continued to isolate myself in my room on the mental ward. I wasn't quite able to come to grips with the idea that I was ill. It was clear to everyone except me that I was not appropriate for the community and may be dangerous without taking medication to turn down the volume of the voices and whispers. The medication had effectively reduced the distress initially accompanied by the voices. But, I could still hear passing whispers as I went through my days. While on medication, they were less pushy. Instead of convincing me that the river valley my parents lived in was about to drown under a sea of rain, the whispers were becoming more random.

For example, I would hear diet suggestions, "Butter," or completely nonsensical words that would just pass through my consciousness like "Grass trimmings."

Chapter Five

I walked up to the nurses' station every morning and afternoon. They handed me two dixie cups, one with a few pills in it, another full of water. I slammed the pills like a shot of fireball on a Friday night. In fact, I would actually imagine I was taking a shot of whiskey just before I tilted my head back to ingest the meds in an effort to simulate enjoyment. But, there was no joy to be had. A gaggle of strippers could have swung their tits from the rafters. It didn't matter. The medication had me doped up in such a way that I didn't have the capacity to experience any real pleasure. I wasn't the only mental patient with diminished cognitive abilities either. It was a full-blown zombie apocalypse situation in there. I guess it's a place where they need to try *some* kind of medication on folks. After all, if you've ended up in a mental ward, the assumption is that you are some flavor of crazy. So, they probably err on the side of too much medication to see some behavioral change.

As soon as I stopped verbally responding to my internal whispers, they started explaining how much progress I'd made. But really, I was so doped up I just didn't give a fuck about responding. I slobbered. That was not an observable behavior the discharge planner or psychiatrist was concerned about. Subtly moving my lips in response to the internal whispers was unacceptable. Slobbering all over myself and pissing my pants while sleeping, half-sleeping, because I didn't have the energy to walk to the bathroom was a 'normal part of the recovery process'.

The best psychiatrists are genuinely curious to hear how the experience takes form in the individual's consciousness. They don't pretend to know what a schizophrenic is going through. But, I wasn't interested in being authentic with shrinks. I learned how to manipulate on a different level during this three-week stay in the Spokane County Evaluation and Treatment Center. It was pretty clear what they were looking for: the patient to swallow pills, sleep, and follow their directions. I complied, I got discharged.

Chapter Six

My parents picked me up on the day I was discharged. It was humiliating. I could tell how my dad was speaking to me that he had changed the way he thought about me. When I spoke to him, my mind's eye was blinded by the glare of a foreign dynamic in our relationship. This dynamic made it difficult to speak with him. Looking at this objectively through the lens of a different stage of life may be impossible, but I still believe the pharmaceuticals in my system were so heavily prescribed at that time, I couldn't keep up with a conversation. But I could see that my dad spoke to me differently than he had in the past. He used an artificially cheerful tone. I was essentially being prompted to do everything. You know, like a mental patient.

"Why don't you hop in the car, Jack, and we'll get ya back to civilization," my dad sounded like a grade school teacher prodding a six-year-old back into the classroom after recess.

I wanted to insult him for speaking to me that way, but I was incapable of exchanging jabs in a lucid fashion as my brain was fogged over. This fog covered up the voices to a certain degree, but it also zapped my ability to think quickly or even react naturally with emotion. The idea that I had lost his respect, that he no longer loved me the same as he had before my mental break, made me feel like a failure. It made me want to get off the meds so I could speak with him normally again, so I could gain back his respect, his love.

It's about a three-hour drive east from Spokane to my folks' house in Wenatchee. I wish I could say that the car was filled with awkward silence. Instead, I blabbered like a drunken buffoon to regain lost respect. As opposed to awkward silence, the car was bursting with the desperation of a lost soul. The small amount of self-esteem I still had, I hung onto by my fingertips, and then released during this humiliating trip.

"How are you doing yourself, Dad?" A desperate move to divert attention away from myself.

"I'm doing fine, Jack, don't worry about me. Your mom and I are concerned about you. We want to help you."

I started plotting my escape during the ride back to Wenatchee. I would take one of their vehicles as soon as the opportunity presented itself. My destination was to be determined, along with how I would fund the escapade. That part was not vital. I was now functioning under the relative stability of the antipsychotics I had been prescribed in the mental ward, so I could operate within reasonable proximity of reality.

However, I had no intention of continuing the medication after returning to the community. Furthermore, I knew my folks had no chance to detect my cheeking of the medication. In the facility, it was obvious when I tried to cheek the pills. I rolled them under my tongue and swallowed. No dice, they had me lift my tongue at the nurses' station, and I couldn't get away with that shit. But my folks wouldn't even consider the possibility that I was pretending to take the meds and disposing of them. The disposal part could be a bit tricky. You would think that a person may just slip the pills into their pocket and get rid of them later. That doesn't work; they just melt into the pant pockets and become obvious when my mother did laundry. At a certain point, I would start inserting them into my rectum, but it turns out they absorb into the bloodstream just fine via the butthole. In fact, I found out later that certain people with mental illness ingest the meds via the butthole all the time because they have trouble swallowing. Or at least one guy.

At any rate, I was searching for ways to avoid taking the meds because I believed they made me unable to think or function at my highest level. I believed they were poisoning me. Not an uncommon concern from the perspective of a mental patient. Sure, some folks avoid the meds because of delusional influences. But, it's also true that the pharmaceutical industry controls what shrinks prescribe. The meds they make available are the ones they can make the most money off. Obvious, but worth pointing out.

Over the next week, I avoided ingesting the meds without any suspicion. By the end of that week, I needed to be a thousand miles away from my folk's house. My skin was tingling with excitement when I realized I was almost gone. But, I started to hear the whispers speaking much more clearly to me again. They were becoming much more direct. I was also beginning to make loose connections and interpret what they said in strange ways. I knew they were having more influence over me again, but I could also feel my mind starting to function normally. My thoughts may have been delusional, but I could process thoughts quickly once again, and that feeling was liberating. Then suddenly, I received a directive from the voices telling me to grab keys, jump in a car and drive to my old apartment. The apartment I shared with a couple of other jagoffs less than two months earlier.

I had been living a completely different life then. It seemed simultaneously like yesterday and a world away. I hadn't even spoken to those gluttons, but I was pretty sure they would accept me back with the open arms of a substance-fueled celebration. Surely, they would listen to me, empathize with shitty luck and laugh their asses off at the bizarreness of the journey I had just completed. Just a couple minor details to sort out.

My biggest problem was that I didn't have access to any money or a bank account, for that matter. Previously, I was attending university, and my folks were depositing money in an account every month for me to live off. But after everything I had been through in the past couple of months, I had no idea where that bank card was or if there would be money in the account. The dearth of funds was my primary concern. However, this was not enough to deter me from going for broke, or just being broke on the run, as it were.

The opportunities to snatch a set of keys and just leave were available. I felt suspense and excitement knowing that I was about to make an aggressive move toward independence. It tickled a part of my brain that had not been stimulated since I entered the mental facility. I knew my folks would be upset about this, which I considered briefly but dismissed.

The urge to take control of my own destiny, misguided as this internal charge was, could not be stopped by my inhibition. So, as the wild hair in my ass could not be contained, I was off. It was noon on a Thursday. My parents had left me alone in the house and headed to Home Depot to pick out some new curtains. I had manipulated them into thinking that I was compliant. Compliant with the treatment, the meds, and the entire assumption that I recognized I had an illness to manage.

Chapter Seven

I headed west from Wenatchee en route for Seattle on I-90. I hadn't been behind the wheel in a while, and the buzz I was feeling from the moment's excitement was somewhat intoxicating. I focused hard on staying in my lane during that little joy ride. Cruise control helped maintain a speed that would not get me pulled over. As far as I knew, I hadn't broken any laws yet, as long as my folks hadn't reported the car stolen. Which they probably did. I proceeded. It's about a three-hour drive. I can recall driving across Lake Washington as I approached Seattle's skyline. It seemed like God had placed a spotlight on my parents' Subaru hatchback. A gleaming star traveling across the lake. Grandiosity may be too light of a term to describe what I felt.

I circled the block around the apartment building just west of the university. I had shared the unit with two other dudes I had met freshman year. They were nothing more than drinking buddies, though. I couldn't wait to see those fucking guys. I decided I would lie about where I had been all this time. I would tell them that I'd gone on a last-minute trip through Europe. That I suddenly got the urge to travel, took out a credit card, and kept going until I hit the max. No need to explain any further. They would respect the independent free spirit of such a journey and begin to view me as a more cultured individual. Perhaps I had started out in Paris, where I hooked up with a middle-eastern broad. It didn't really matter. These dopes will buy whatever I had to sell. I found a parking spot on the street and marched up the steps toward the apartment with the blind confidence of a lunatic. I knew the door would be unlocked, so I walked right in.

"Jack?"

"Bryan, my man. How are things?"

"What are you doing here, Jack?"

"Ahhh... I fucking live here. I realize I've been away for a bit. But I'm back. Nice to see you too." I could feel the humiliation already.

"Are you ok, man? I mean, what happened?"

Bryan spoke to me with an awkward tone. It triggered me to defend myself. So, I spewed the bullshit about an impulsive European trip to fill the space of time I had been away from them. Hard to say how long I rambled at them, pleading for acceptance, dripping with desperation. They knew I was lying but didn't know what to say, so they let me continue the incoherent blabbing.

"I got the urge to just get out of here for a while, so I pretty much just took out a credit card and flew to Europe. I had the time of my life," a shameless lie, of course. Plus, Bryan and the other jerkoff friends I had must have known I had been caged up in the university police station jail, crazy as a lune. But for some reason, I didn't want to admit that to myself. I wanted to believe that somehow I could just fly back into my former life under the radar.

"Look, Jack, we know you were in a mental hospital. Your dad called here and told us what was going on. He also just called me an hour ago, saying you might show up here. He said you've been back at their house for a couple weeks since being discharged and that you might not be on your meds," Bryan informed with an offensive tone.

It was painful to hear that my father had colluded against me. That he had suspected I was off my meds and still didn't confront me while I was in his house. It was my dad's fault. I felt abandoned by him. He didn't even respect me or care enough about me to ask me if I was taking the meds. I was also upset with him for wanting me to take meds in the first place, so none of it made any sense. I was mentally decompensating, and my perception was a far cry from reality. I stood speechless and humiliated in the living room of my old apartment. My old roommates stared back at me like I was a lost toddler who ran off on a conniption fit, wandering around in search of something that doesn't exist, clueless.

I bolted from the apartment, jumped back in my parent's Subaru, and moved it several blocks away. I really wasn't familiar with Seattle generally, other than the university district. I had spent virtually all my time on the campus or within a few blocks. I ended up staying in the car overnight. My situation, in reality, grew increasingly isolated. My psychosis was gradually building stronger between my ears. What I mean is, the voices got louder, more aggressive. I was dealing with a full-blown untreated mental illness. The following day I walked around campus, looking for someone I knew as a student. Someone to stay with. In doing so, I began to feel further isolated as I realized that I didn't have any close relationships on the campus at all. I was alone.

I walked back to the Subaru to get a slice of privacy and found that it was towed. My parents had reported the vehicle stolen, and now I had nowhere to hide, no shelter from the rain. I had nothing but auditory hallucinations to keep me company. I had less than nothing, a deficit. So I continued down the university way, past the homeless kids I had purchased drugs from them a couple months earlier, and began to realize I was almost one of them. I spotted the salesman who appeared to manage the group. Any business seemed to go through him. He saw me coming down the block and was probably drawn by the desperation dripping off me. I was an easy mark. Primed for him to catch in his web. I had nowhere to turn, a distorted sense of reality, and a motivation to engage in illicit drug activity.

"How ya doin buddy? My name's Tex." An interesting question for me to contemplate at that moment, phrased very appropriately by Tex.

I could see that Tex was taking advantage of vulnerable youth on the street. Even in my compromised state. I didn't care. It was the furthest thing from my mind. I was now only concerned about meeting my own basic needs and no longer had room for social justice issues. I slipped into a state of survival. And for some reason, my ego, along with the voices, would not allow me to consider contacting my parents.

"I need something to eat. Do you have any food?" I continued, dripping with desperation.

"Sure thing, buddy. Just come along with me, and I'll get you fixed right up," Tex assured me.

Chapter Eight

Due to the large population of homeless youth in the U District and the large population of bleeding heart liberals, there are a lot of social services available to help these kids. I was nineteen and technically an adult, but many of these services work with kids up to age twenty-four. Tex had found a way to tap into this market and was playing this population on both ends. Taking advantage of them on one end by getting them drug-addicted and dependent on him; and on the other hand, helping them meet their own basic needs. He became my only friend very quickly.

Tex walked me to a food bank/shelter for homeless young adults. I showered, ate some shitty food, and fell asleep on a floor mat. Being thrown into a group of troubled, homeless young adults allowed me to basically blend right into the crowd. The kids in this shelter arrived there by many different routes; aged out of the foster system, running from predators elsewhere. And there were undoubtedly many others who had recently experienced the onset of a psychotic disorder staying under the same roof, sleeping feet away from me on a mat. Listening to the voices inside their heads, as I was.

Being herded together into a flock of crazy, heroin-addicted fuck-ups made for a great deal of anonymity. Everyone was only concerned with getting dope and surviving. They couldn't plan anything because they didn't have any control over their lives. Life was in control of them. I stayed at the shelter for about one week without speaking more than a couple of words to anyone. They make everyone leave at 6 am, and the doors open back up at 6 pm. I spent those days underneath overpasses and wandering through the campus I had been attending earlier in the year. I was one of the street kids hovering around the margins of the University of Washington undergrad population.

In addition to the marginalization, I was decompensating to the point where the whispers were difficult to tease out again. Surely, I was becoming difficult to recognize as a sane person. Time quickly passed. One day, I recall walking past my old roommate, Bryan. I intentionally made eye contact with him, and he didn't even recognize me. I was playing beer pong with this jerkoff a couple months before.

Basically, I was scraping along the bottom of society and collecting enough debris in the process to make me completely unrecognizable. Even by the people I had been closest with just months prior. I was disheveled, unkempt, clothed with handouts from a donation bin, a total mess. The distressed look on my face probably took a much different form than the smug, privileged expression I graced the world with in my previous life.

For whatever reason, I turned inward during this, my second journey into psychosis. I was not being influenced to divert a catastrophic disaster. But the whispers were significant. Perhaps a bit of depression was setting in as well. The disorganization of my thought process made it so. I could barely communicate with anyone about anything. I couldn't track a conversation without becoming distracted enough for my eyes to wander into the sky. I was lost in a rat maze and couldn't focus enough on realizing it. I just kept going back to the shelter at night, taking the food they gave me, waking up, and circling the campus on foot until I became hungry enough to quit. Subsequently, I would walk back to the shelter. I had no other options that I was aware of, and my mind had turned down a road where I no longer had any thoughts of my parents.

Soon enough, Tex resurfaced. "Hey, bud, how ya holding up?"

Even in the throes of psychosis, I knew that Tex didn't have my best interests in mind. However, I couldn't help but engage with him. He presented himself as an ally, briefly checking in with me or saying hello almost daily, and I was lonely. I felt rejected, and I had begun to contemplate whether it was worth it to continue on this path. Contacting my parents wasn't an option. I couldn't stand to see my father again. I wasn't going to be any kind of burden or visible disappointment to anyone. I was at the peak of my vulnerability. Each day, as I wandered around in my own little world, I would cross the freeway overpass, and the thought of throwing myself over the edge to just end this suffering became more appealing. Tex was aware of my desperation. He had an understanding of the type of illness I was dealing with. He'd been watching me from afar. He saw how poorly I was doing and wanted to get to me before I either killed myself or got connected to some sort of caseworker. After allowing me to hover over the edge of life for several weeks, Tex eventually approached me. He put his hand on my shoulder and gently made eye contact. He seemed empathetic to my situation without saying a word.

"Hey," I dully replied as if my life up to that point hadn't occurred, and my expectations were based on this moment alone. I was like a beetle on the sidewalk, creeping along, just waiting to get scooped up by a bird or something. Tex was that bird. Perhaps it was just reality, humanity, natural selection in action.

"How are they treating you over at the shelter?" Tex inquired.

"Ok."

"If you wanna come check out where I stay, I'll show you. I camp over by the 520 bridge, in the arboretum," Tex offered.

"Ok."

The arboretum is a large wooded area adjacent to the University of Washington campus. It takes up a large swath of land along Lake Washington. Highway 520, a bridge that crosses Lake Washington, also crosses through the arboretum, providing a lot of cover with a variety of nooks and crannies for people who have been pushed to the margins of the community to seek shelter. In combination, the highway overpass and the wooded arboretum provide a great deal of privacy. A lot of campsite options for transient homeless folks.

During my stay in the shelter, my daily ritual of pacing around the neighborhood took me right through Tex's location, where his camp of lost, homeless souls resided. The plant growth in the arboretum is so thick that I never noticed an encampment. They could have jumped right out of the bush and bit me in the ass. I would never have seen them coming.

Chapter Nine

The arboretum is a microcosm of humanity: Subsets of people moving through, ignoring each other. A group of affluent gay men walking on the trail, chatting. They pass by a group of college students, stoned as fuck, tossing a Frisbee around. A single mother sits on a blanket in the grass under the shade of an evergreen, with her two sons who will grow up without a father and take that frustration out on every authority figure they cross along the way. Just a few yards away, tucked behind overgrown bushes, around the side of a park service building, a group of homeless young adults herd together like penguins on the Discovery Channel. About twenty of them in all. A pretty even split between male and female, racially diverse.

"I got an extra tent for ya," Tex informed me.

It wasn't difficult to recruit me. He could've offered a handful of goose shit for a snack, and I would have been agreeable. Tex assigned a camp member to help me put up the tent. I slept in the tent the first night without a sleeping bag or any blankets. Nothing. In a way, being inside the tent made me feel sheltered from the whispers. Or at least as though the whispers were being strained through a filter. Camping in this setting was very dangerous, but that reality hadn't occurred to me. The tent gave me a false sense of security. It didn't take long for Tex to drop off a sleeping bag for me, and pretty soon, I was relatively comfortable.

I continued to get meals from the same food bank, connected to the shelter I stayed at before moving to Tex's camp at the arboretum. During my first week at the encampment, I hardly spoke to a soul. The other campers seemed to isolate themselves in their tents as well. For me, part of the virtue of this living environment was the tribal setting without a sense of community. Little communication took place between residents of this neighborhood of tents. I certainly was not interested in conversing with my neighbors. I wasn't interested in conversing with anyone at first. I was over a month into homelessness. I was distracted by the whispers to such a degree that my ability to communicate verbally with anyone was extremely limited. The life I had led for the past nineteen years had been cleaned off the slate. I had no form of identification, no form of currency, and no explanation for how I ended up in this situation. I was navigating through a disorganized, dysfunctional mind, unable to recognize myself, a lost soul.

The tents sat on pallets to lift them above soggy ground very effectively. Surprisingly, pallets are readily available as well. Totally untapped resource. You can snag up free pallets behind any Home Depot. Driving through any industrial district will reveal the vastness of this resource. Planet earth is lousy with pallets. The only people who get proper use of stray pallets are homeless campers. It's astonishing what a homeless heroin addict with a background in general construction can do with an unlimited supply of pallets. Tex had me ride with this guy late at night to circle around a Home Depot in West Seattle and toss a bunch of pallets into the truck. We brought them back to the campsite, which was slowly expanding.

I had settled into a bit of a routine that included daily substance use, of course, provided by Tex. Pain pills and daily alcohol consumption were somewhat effective in helping me tolerate my whispers. Or at least allowing me to ignore them while I was loaded. I was able to function again, using booze and pain pills to self-medicate. A small hit of cocaine occurred, but not daily. It was more of a tool used when an objective was at hand. If physical effort would be required to complete vital tasks, cocaine was used to stimulate the effort. I always took a hit of crack right before we left to go pick up pallets. I needed it to offset the fatigue of heroin use. Crack isn't my drug of choice at all, just a tool to help complete tasks.

The camp was lousy with bent spoons and used needles – the standard of life. The heroin looked like condensed cat shit, mixed with water and boiled with a lighter underneath a bent tablespoon. But at this point, I still wasn't injecting,

47

only smoking the stuff. When people ask me why I tried heroin in the first place, I have trouble answering. I was generally indifferent to the world at the time. Looking for a way to escape the noise in my head. I was not worried about what consequence my behavior could lead to. I definitely wasn't worried about becoming a junkie. I had no reason NOT to give it a try. One thing is for sure: while I was on heroin, I was not thinking about killing myself.

Maybe, in some dark corner of my mind, I knew it could provide some relief. The underbelly of society where I found myself provided a place to exist but with little pleasure. The folks in this encampment were barely surviving. Anything to relieve a bit of stress, take an edge off, or provide some type of distraction was appealing. The arboretum campsite was occupied exclusively by heroin users. I had enough sense to know that injecting this drug would be going down a rabbit hole I may never climb out of, and I resisted as long as I could. But smoking that stuff provides its own disgusting challenges. The first time I injected heroin was a few weeks into my stay at the campsite. Tex came into my tent with a store-bought container of hot soup and offered me heroin with it. A hot meal that was not from the food bank was very appealing. Of course, Tex knew that I was not an injection drug user at that point. The soup is what pushed me over the edge. I wanted it badly.

"Hey Jack, I have some soup here and also brought you a bag."

"What kind of bag?" I asked.

"Heroin. I figure you could use a good night's sleep, buddy."

Tex loaded up a rig, getting it ready to inject me for the first time as if we did it often. He boiled it up in a bent spoon and filtered it out with some cotton, ensuring I was paying attention to the process. Tex injected my first hit of heroin into the vein running over my right wrist. The feeling of euphoria was immediate, stronger than when I had smoked it. I was relaxed, and the torture of my existence had found a respite. I tried to stay awake because I didn't want to end the experience. It had a grip on me right away. As soon as that hypodermic needle released the opiate into my bloodstream, my brain fell in love with the substance in a new way.

The cost for my heroin was free in the arboretum encampment, supplied by Tex. I functioned well enough to continue living, and the heroin prevented me from submitting to a psychiatric crisis, numbing my brain like the psych meds had done in Spokane. So, for a moment in time at the arboretum, life was enjoyable. I developed a strong connection with the other campers, despite our non-verbal nature. Most of us had a lot of internal dialogue, and we lacked the time or motivation to chat with each other. This was understood. Body language was enough. But, I did feel supported. We were a pack of something. You could say we resembled dogs, penguins, whatever. From my vantage point, meerkats are the most accurate description of what we were. Silently scanning the perimeter of the campsite, huddling together when danger approached. Otherwise, occupied by our own thoughts and working to isolate ourselves from other species. Maybe that's just the way I view meerkats. Perhaps it's a common misconception, and really, they are more aggressive in their behavior. However, the perception of the folks in our encampment was not a misconception. We had no desire to communicate with the outside world.

We were marginalizing ourselves. I'm not sure if society was doing it to us. Perhaps there should have been a service to better engage us back into the community. At any rate, we were the meerkats of humanity. Very vulnerable targets, but with safeguards in place. We were afraid of conflict but not afraid to huddle ourselves together, hide behind anything. We weren't much to anyone, similar to meerkats who don't have much meat on their bones. We didn't have any money or utility. We were there, occupying a bit of oxygen, hiding in the tunnels.

I was caught staring at another one of the campers several times as we milled around the campsite. She was somehow beautiful despite her condition. She ended up paying me a visit to ask if I had any clean needles like a cup of sugar in suburbia or something. I hadn't felt normal anxiety for a while until I found myself scrambling around my tent in search of her requested needle. It took me a while. I finally pulled it out of a thrift store duffle bag. She sat down in my tent. She seemed lonely, suppressed, but she looked like she had been a talkative person in a previous life. Her name was Maggie.

"Do you usually shoot up alone?" she asked delicately.

"Yeah, I do. But Tex shoots me up some of the time cause I haven't done it much."

"That's the way he was with me. I've been staying here for a couple months since I aged out of the foster system."

"What do you mean?"

"I turned eighteen, and the family I was staying with stopped getting paid by the state. So they dropped me off at a shelter in the U District. I was there for a bit before Tex offered me a spot here." Her story was identical to mine.

"That's how I met him. I ended up in the shelter after losing my mind, though."

"What do you mean losing your mind?"

"I started hearing these whispers, and now I don't know what the fuck is real or not sometimes. I can hear them in the back of my head right now." She nodded with understanding as I spoke, which normalized it for me somehow. All of a sudden, I felt less ashamed of my whispers.

"Oh yeah, he likes to bring in schizophrenics. It seems like you are dealing with them ok though."

"Honestly, the heroin helps me ignore them."

"Yeah, it kind of has that effect. I can pretty much ignore the entire world when I'm doped up, a world I'm choosing not to face." I felt a certain type of validation from Maggie right away. She understood my circumstance more, given her history and life experience. She also helped me realize that I was actually lucky in many ways, too. I didn't have to deal with an endless series of foster parents providing shelter for money, along with many types of abuse throughout her life. And an overall lack of love, which I couldn't understand at all. She made me think of my parents.

Chapter Ten

Maggie and I started to spend most of our waking hours together, which were not many. Maybe a five-hour window of time per day during which we could communicate without the daze of heroin sedation or opiate-induced coma-sleep. We developed a strong connection and began to consider each other partners in a relationship. Sex was difficult to execute, given the effect heroin has on body function generally. Perhaps we were seduced by heroin into the allusion of love. So, the sex wasn't always great, but it was phenomenal when we were sober enough to feel the sensation. We handled each other well.

Maggie was an athletically built 5'7" with a great bust, supple, tender breasts falling off her body like they were designed by a perverted god. Her hair was dark brown, thick all the way to her sleek collar bone. Light, soft skin. She typically wore her hair in a ponytail, occasionally letting it down to reveal her classy beauty. Her eyes were brown and bright, instantly drawing me in. Her lips were the softest tissue I'd ever touched. She was beautiful. I imagined being married to her, having money, and taking her out to a lavish dinner somewhere downtown. She would make everyone look bad. Even without a spec of makeup, she was incredible.

Maggie and I rarely got completely naked inside our skimpy tent, which was the only place available to us for intimate activity. This was between December and January. We were bundled up in hoodies and snow pants to stay warm. We had several dirty comforter blankets taken from local clothing banks as well. So, it was a laborious task for us to have sex, given the physical circumstances and the effects of heroin coursing through our veins. So, we held each other, dry-humped, and figured out how to get each other off despite the unromantic setting. Eventually, we progressed into regular sexual activity. The morning worked for us, before we shot up for the day.

I enjoyed pleasuring Maggie. Our strong sexual attraction was reciprocal. Being intimate with Maggie in the morning was more addictive than our afternoon heroin usage. We initiate with tender kissing as we tickled each other erotically. We knew where each other's sensitive areas were, and both stimulated with delicate skill. We had a very complementary taste. Neither of us was looking for something aggressive. Delicate lovers.

Her vagina throbbed as she began to demand soft, quick movements on her clitoris. I'd try to produce stringy saliva to stimulate her nipples, and her back would arch. Her body trembled like something was trying to get out of it. Our clothes were generally on during this playtime, pants unbuttoned. Our hands were burrowed under each other's garments, which somehow added an additional tantalizing layer of erotica. We were living like scum, but it was a high quality of life, for a slice of time. Maggie returned the favor well. We both enjoyed the give and take.

There's something about the manual labor aspect of a handjob I appreciate. It can't be enjoyable to handle a penis like that. Hammering a nail through the drywall into a stud. It's hard to cum on heroin. A good time to elicit a handjob for me was right after waking up. That way, Maggie didn't have to jerk me off forever and then have me fail to ejaculate. It was better than sex. Maggie has finesse, and she brought me right to the edge of the cliff, backed me off, and continued to softly tease me with the elusive orgasm. Using her own slimy saliva as a lubricant, she stroked with grace in a natural motion. Until finally, she would let me shoot off the edge of the cliff and tumble into a canyon of fluffy pillows. In reality, I was laying on a thin layer of vinyl between my ass cheeks and a soggy pallet, inside a musty, disgusting tent littered with dirty needles. But somehow, it was beautifully erotic. Again, heroin.

Maggie and I got the bag of black tar heroin from Tex each day around 2 pm, right as we started to feel dope sick, experience withdrawal symptoms, and our bodies demanded the fix. Tex made sure we were desperate before he arrived at our tent zipper to drop it off. We were enslaved by the needle, by Tex. This was life. After waking up in the morning and occasionally enjoying a seductive hand job, we walked about half a mile out of the arboretum, to the youth shelter near the university campus to eat. The shelter served daily meals to homeless youth whether they stayed in the shelter or not. This was our only meal for the day. We typically left with a jug of water and some replacement syringes from the needle exchange. Although, Maggie and I often ended up sharing needles when we inevitably ran out. We would return to our campsite, pathetically searching the trail for cigarette butts that may have a drag left, and approach the campsite with shame, scanning the area, hoping that no one would see us navigate the pile of human waste to enter our tent. We just kept up this routine, thinking that eventually cops would show up and force us to move on, or arrest us for creating a public health hazard in such a beautiful park, like the arboretum.

"How long do you think we can stay here like this?" I asked Maggie as we stepped over rotting garbage to unzip our tent.

"As long as Tex keeps us here, under his spell," she replied with a hopeless spirit.

As the days trudged by, it became clear that Tex was taking advantage of me, and the rest of us. However, I still didn't give a shit. I knew he was holding me in his bullpen. I didn't know what my utility was. I just wanted to continue staying there and use free heroin. In fact, I would do anything to continue doing the same thing. He had me. I was addicted to the heroin he was supplying. I was staying in the campsite he funded, that he sanctioned. I realized everyone there was in the same situation. A bunch of lunes chomping at the bit for the next hit of black tar.

Not everyone was schizophrenic, though, but a good majority were. We definitely had some folks with developmental disabilities who were now dependent on heroin. Collectively, we were obviously vulnerable. Some of the campers at this site barely even left. I would say around half of the folks even traveled to a toilet when they had to shit, which wasn't often on account of the heroin plugging up their guts.

It was probably just a matter of time until someone overdosed. Eventually, it happened to a guy who had slammed the full three-gram supply from Tex all at once. His name was Chip, and he shared a tent with his girlfriend, Franky. The two of them had been staying there for a couple of months after being indoctrinated by Tex. After the body was discovered, someone called 911, and I was roused awake by a cop inside my tent.

"Please get yourself together. We would like to talk to you, son." I was ushered to a Seattle PD van, where I was wrapped in a blanket. I could see Franky speaking with a couple of cops, crying. The cops began asking me questions about Tex.

"How did you meet Tex?" I was a bit disorganized and unable to provide detailed answers. But, I could tell that they were focused on Tex.

"Has he ever forced himself on you?"

"What does that mean?"

"Did Tex ever force you to have sex with him?"

"No. I don't think so."

Tex was nowhere to be found. The campsite was being broken down by the cops. My fellow campers and I were beginning to withdraw. We had been corralled into a few different vans, and the cops were trying to run us for warrants. Which was difficult for them to do because virtually none of us had any ID. I provided a false last name and date of birth. I could hear Franky speaking angrily with the cops in the background.

"He murdered him! He did it on purpose! He knew that was too much to inject, and then he raped him after he was out!"

As I rode to King County Jail in the back of a police van, I wondered if Tex had raped me. He definitely injected me a number of times. Each time I passed out hard, it would have been easy for him to have his way with me. Maggie pulled me away from the noise and whispered in my ear.

"Tex raped me too, Jack, when I first got here. He injected me and then raped me. That's why I wanted to sleep in your tent at first. But then I fell in love with you," Maggie explained with distress. I didn't hold it against her. I also didn't know what the fuck was going on.

I may have exchanged more dialogue with my fellow arboretum campers on the way to the jail than I had during my two-month residency. Maggie was distraught. She just sat next to me, sobbing. She couldn't stand to hear the stories from others. The consensus view was that it was common practice for Tex to inject one of his campers with a large enough amount of heroin to allow him to have sexual intercourse while they were unconscious. Against their unknowing wills.

By the time we arrived at the jail, everyone in the police van was in shock. Not just because we were all entering into the initial stages of heroin withdrawal, but we were about to be locked up. The numbing effect that the heroin had on my whispers was already wearing off. I was terrified of the probability that I had been raped in my sleep. Males *and* females had reported rape during the ride. Apparently, Tex swang from both sides regarding his gender preference during a sexual assault.

So, while in jail, I faced a new set of challenges: coping with oncoming whispers and the withdrawal symptoms resulting from my heroin use. The whispers predictably came back with an evil tone when I was behind bars. Very difficult to cope with. My brain chemistry was swinging back in the wrong direction. I was equipped to ride this wave of distress, I felt at the time. Remaining silent to the world was the central principle of my coping strategy at that point, hiding my illness from the world. The van arrived at the jail, and I realized I was once again completely on my own to deal with my whispers. No more heroin.

I was able to repeat the false name I had provided to the cops at the campsite when I arrived at the jail, "Jack Nicholson," which would become my go-to alias. Despite our advanced information age, the same manipulation that worked in the wild west still worked in 2016. I got arrested and lied about my name to avoid identification. They would contact my parents if they knew my true identity. Not to mention my mental health record. I probably would have been sent straight back to the nuthouse if they knew what happened a couple months earlier at the river. However, I was processed in like any other dope-headed heroin bum. The jail nurse asked if I had any abscesses from injecting.

Luckily, I hadn't yet developed any. I was congratulated by the intake nurse.

Chapter Eleven

I sat in jail for a couple days on a trespassing charge, listening to my whispers fester and wondering if I would ever see Maggie again. I missed her enormously and wanted to sink into her arms. This would have been a great opportunity to reconnect with my family and seek treatment. However, that option didn't even cross my mind. The whispers grew louder with the absence of heroin in my system. I became increasingly paranoid, fearing the world was after me somehow. I needed to disguise my existence to avoid its detection. When I was doped up, I couldn't give a shit. I sank into an opiate-induced mind-space where I could close my eyes and float through the universe. Not in jail. It was awful.

Sitting in a jail cell, once again, listening to my voices sing chorus songs, I scanned the room to see if anyone was staring at me, if they knew I was crazy.

"You look like you dope sick, eh, bruh?" asked a well-kempt, good-looking African American guy in his mid-twenties.

"What? Oh yeah, you nailed it," I responded, unsure at first if he was speaking to me as my voices were distracting me at that moment. I looked over at him, made eye contact for a moment, and tried to track what he was saying as words sprayed from his mouth like a firehose.

"Damn boy, you might be crazy for real. And dope sick. Tell you what, my name is Alvin. I'll hang with yo ass. You ain't got to say a word, bro," Alvin seemed to be interested in watching after me. Perhaps I needed that. Maybe it was obvious. Soon we were moved from our atrium cell to eat lunch. We sat at a table in a large mess hall, Alvin talking circles around the voices in my head, me staring at him, wondering what the fuck he was talking about. Seemed like a nice enough guy, though.

"You got track marks running up your arm like a fuckin NASCAR event, bruh," Alvin observed, "I can get you some dope when we out of here, or pills if you want to stop injecting, but that will cost you more. You seem like you're good for it, good lookin' white dude like yourself." Alvin was obviously interested in selling me drugs.

"I already got a guy. Or I did. He might be in jail for a while if they find him." I responded with basic information, which was about as much as I could provide at the time.

"Oh, you got a guy? What's his name?"

"Tex."

"Bahah! You kiddin', right?" Alvin's vociferous personality filled the large room as he burst into laughter. "That creepy motherfucker is still around town, eh? Shit, watch out for him. Hey man, do you know who Tex gets his dope from?"

"I have no idea," I responded.

The jail guards rounded us up like a herd of cats and returned us to the atrium cell, which held a group of us, non-violent types. Alvin continued to recruit addicts as if the jail was a convention hall and he was advertising his services to potential clients. I sat wondering if my false identity would hold up. It seemed way too easy to just feed them a fake name. But I was just some street kid, without an ID, who just got dragged into jail from a campsite. That's who I am, nobody. No family, nothing.

They didn't keep me in jail for very long. I got out of it without any drug charges, trespassing only. The lawyer said the cops were distracted by the dead guy and didn't bother to sort out who slept in which tent. So, even though the campsite was littered with needles, spoons, and black tar, none of the arboretum residents were charged with possession. My hearing at King County court lasted only a few minutes, and I was able to get through it with a 'yes ma'am' approach as directed by my public defender.

This was the first offense of any kind for my alias: Jack Nicholson. Although I got off with just a trespassing violation, the judge strongly suggested Mr. Nicholson seek treatment. But I was not given any options for accessing such a thing. So even if I was interested in treatment, it wasn't possible to get into a program. It was surprising how easily

I was able to create a new identity. I didn't get the impression that anyone gave a shit whether I was lying or not. Just another homeless heroin addict in a city littered with thousands of them. That was my identity to the court system. A life that was destined to circle the city's drain and end up clogging it. Like a ball of dead hair jamming up the drain, making it so the rest of the discarded filth can't be flushed into the sewer. I was worth less than nothing, and that was their expectation for me. However, I now had fingerprints in the system to identify me, so I couldn't create more pseudo names after getting arrested. I was released to the street from King County Jail, located in downtown Seattle. As I mentioned earlier, I wasn't very familiar with downtown at the time, having spent virtually all of my time in the University District several miles away, which includes the arboretum.

So, I wandered downtown for a couple days, becoming increasingly psychotic and desperate to get my hands on some heroin. It was difficult to avoid getting picked back up by the police simply because they put me in the position upon release from jail. As soon as I sat down for a rest, whether in a park or on a street bench, whatever, they were all over me like a cheap suit. Basically, it was illegal to be homeless with nowhere to go. Or that's what it felt like. They had to be able to tell how psychotic I was, the cops. Even if they cared enough to help me, I wasn't open to it. The whispers were telling me – in so many words – that everyone was trying to torture me. The fact that my reality was reinforcing this perception was not helpful. I needed a nice injection to quiet down the voices. Heroin was everywhere.

Other homeless guys were milling around everywhere with that particular glaze in their eyes. Having a hard time keeping their eyes open while they walked down the sidewalk. Like me, they were trying not to get arrested for existing. What I needed was all around me. The problem was that I was so compromised by the whispers that I couldn't engage in a meaningful conversation. I wasn't able to walk up to a dope dealer and say, "Can I get a bag, please?" Why the fuck couldn't I just ask someone? Fuck! I was already desperate for heroin, so it's not like a dealer would give me a bag just to hook me on the stuff. I was already hooked.

Lucky me, I wandered into an oasis. I had ventured into the margins of the city, back to the unsanctioned, sovereign world of homeless human herds. I suppose a gaggle might be a better term to define a human homeless encampment. It roughly resembled a group of gorillas in an actual jungle. Anyway, I ended up heading in that direction in a predictable fashion. The cops had essentially pushed me into the dark corners of the city under the threat of incarceration. They pushed me out like a labrador on a pheasant hunt. On my way out of downtown, I spotted a couple of guys who were obviously campers themselves. I guess at this point, I had developed some instincts that applied to street life. These two middle-aged, homeless guys looked like they could lead me somewhere other than jail. I followed them as they methodically navigated through a couple of fence lines underneath I-5. Exhausted, I couldn't keep up with them. I hadn't eaten for almost two full days, and I was beginning to get weak. So they lost me. But, I was able to follow the stench and stumbled my way into an encampment, deeply hidden under this green belt of urban forest just east of downtown. It's encased by I-5 and sealed off from the rest of society. A lawless village in the underbelly of Seattle.

Part II: The Jungle

Canto I

Locally it's called 'the jungle'. Imagine three thousand homeless people camping in various conditions of shelter. The western border of the jungle is less than a mile from downtown Seattle. This was a very dangerous place, and I stumbled in as an easy mark. Too easy. Which, I believe, was why the matriarch of the jungle stepped in and protected me when I was immediately shaken down like a drunk white man in a Thai brothel. Females were rare in the jungle due to their rough humanity. Like a female in a male prison. So, this was an exceptionally tough and cunning female who could thrive among barbarians.

"You gotta be careful, hon. You look sick as hell." She handed me a bottle of water and sat me down on her tent porch. I was able to get down a banana she offered as well. I think she probably had me diagnosed pretty quick. Her name was Rita, and she saved my life that day. If not for her, I would have been hung out to dry in the literal sense. I woke up wrapped in a motorcycle cover like a cocoon.

"How ya doin', hon? Ya slept for a coons age." The sleep was undoubtedly beneficial to my mental status. I woke up with a window of lucidity.

"I'm ok. Thank you."

Rita had a very warm presence, motherly. She was around fifty years old, Caucasian, somewhat heavy set.

Relatively healthy-looking. So, not a heroin addict. Nope, Rita was a drinker. Drinkers accounted for a pretty good chunk of the population in the jungle. Although the majority of the encampment was occupied by dopeheads like myself.

"So, how long you been dealing with the voices, hon?" Yes, Rita was sharp, had been around the block a few times, and had learned some stuff along the way.

"Not long. Maybe four months, not sure exactly. I can hear the whispers right now."

"Oh, I love how you call em whispers, hon. My son has schizophrenia. So did my daddy."

This was a shot of reality into a bizarre world. She was carrying me along, so I had to listen. Rita could see I couldn't have much of a conversation. I'd decided to trust her despite my paranoia. It was a wise and obvious decision. Without Rita, I was dead in the water. I wouldn't be able to survive on my own, let alone thrive.

"That's what they sound like," I said about the whispers.

"Do they tell ya much? Or just mutter along?"

"They don't say anything specific usually. But together, they kind of encourage me in ways."

"I'll be dipped. That's not much like I've heard before."

Rita was a de facto mental health professional. She grew up around psychosis, raised psychotic kids. She had a pretty sophisticated perspective on mental illness, schizophrenia in particular. My experience of the illness was interesting to her.

"So, you can't really understand what the voices are saying, but you can tell what they want you to do?" she really knew how to cut through the fog.

Rita opened up her family to me – I don't think anyone in this circle was biologically related to her. But this isn't a story about how to define a nuclear family. Rita's tent, which was more of a shack, was a part of a circle of tents. Similar to a wagon circle in the old west. We referred to this circle as *The Ranch*. A pallet trail acted as an entrance to the circle, opposite Rita's shack. So, anytime someone entered the circle, she would see them. The site sat atop a small hill, more of a hump on one side. The other side ran up against an extremely thick swath of shrubbery, which acted as a natural barrier. If someone were approaching the ranch from that direction, they would be making enough of a disruption to easily be detected. The tents were rigged with various barriers to prevent people from walking into the site between them. Chicken wire, even a fence made of upright pallets reinforced by posts, set with concrete mix. The pallet trail entrance was needed due to the muddy condition of the soil, especially at the bottom of the hump. Essentially we were surrounded by a mud mote. The ranch was prime real estate within the jungle.

There were six members of the ranch crew. Everyone took orders from Rita, who was the unquestioned leader, the only female on the ranch. There was a set of twins, Quincy and Clive, who were essentially Rita's secret service detail. They protected her at all costs and looked at her as a motherly type, as we all did. The twins were in their late twenties, African American, and built for conflict. They were only about 5'10 but over 200 pounds, physically imposing. They were damaged souls, as I was, but had found a home under the direction of Rita. They weren't psychotic like I was. Nope, Quincy and Clive's disordered minds were man-made. They experienced the kind of childhood trauma that prevents a person from functioning in the square world. They had grown up locally, in the Rainier Valley section of Seattle. Their mom smoked crack, prostituted herself, and all of the above. The twins were not protected by their mother and were severely abused by a lot of different men. Their mom rented them off to pedophiles to get high many times before they were six years old. So, Quincy and Clive predictably ended up in foster care but were kept together. They lasted in the system until they were about fourteen, when they ran off for good. Of course, the twins had a long history of involvement with the criminal justice system. It's unclear how long they had been staying with Rita, but I think they'd been with her for several years. Rita had provided more care for the twins than anyone else in their lives, and it wasn't close. She managed them well at the stage of life they were stuck in.

You also had Hal. He was about the same age as Rita, a Caucasian, Gulf War veteran. Hal was essentially the maintenance man on the ranch and had constructed what some yuppies would consider being a high-end patio deck out of pallets. It was propped up by posts and Home Depot buckets full of concrete. Stable as a rock. This large circular wooden deck was customized to fit perfectly inside the circular layout of tents that comprised the ranch. In the center of the deck was a circular slot for a burn-barrel with cinder blocks on the ground to prop it up enough to have one foot of the barrel ascending above the deck. Six camping chairs around it. The gaps in the pallets had been filled in with boards from other pallets.

Hal also handled the waste. He had built an outhouse for us on the greenbelt side of the ranch, tucked behind the first layer of trees. He had a system rigged up to catch the shit in a removable bucket and slide it right onto a wheelbarrow. He would dispose of the waste daily and switch out the buckets. I'm not sure where he dumped our shit, but he got rid of it, and that was all the information the other ranch members needed. He collected rainwater, and we were able to use it to take short, very short showers. Hal was also a competent member of Rita's security detail. He was never involved in any territorial enforcement or anything. Physical aggression was a great outlet for the twins, that and booze. So, Rita let Quincy and Clive blow off some steam if anyone needed to get tuned up to protect her business. But, Hal carried a Colt-45 along with the hyper-vigilance of a true combat veteran. He was a constant watchdog, very aware of his surroundings, and ready to protect the ranch at all times.

Hal would actually stagger his sleeping pattern with Donnie, the ranch crew's sixth member, including yours truly. Of course, the staggering sleeping pattern was so that someone was on alert every second throughout the night. Rita was a big target in the jungle, where everyone had a vice. She provided a marketplace for jungle residents to shop for their drug of choice. Often, her customers did not have a form of currency to exchange for their desired product, in which case deals could be made, but were rare. Donnie was a silver-tongued son of a bitch who moved a lot of product for Rita. Donnie was about forty years old, African American. He was living off the grid due to some warrants that would put him away for a long-time. In the jungle, you wouldn't see any milkman making deliveries. However, you would see Donnie making deliveries tent by tent on a daily basis.

It's not as though all 3,000 campers in the jungle purchased substances from the ranch crew. I'm sure some

74

folks carried in product from outside of the jungle. But, Rita would not allow any other dealers to operate within her territory. If someone was reported to have been dealing within the boundaries, they would get a visit from the twins. Furthermore, the ranch armory included a number of firearms. Most of the folks residing in the jungle were heroin junkies who could not own a gun for very long. Not to generalize, but a gun only lasts with a heroin addict until they are out of money. At that point, it gets traded in for a dime bag of black tar.

The primary five members of the ranch crew had clearly defined roles. They operated as a unit and supported each other well. I'm not sure why they accepted me so graciously. Rita began nurturing right away. Helping me deal with the whispers and develop real-life coping skills. Rita knew I wanted to get into her heroin supply, that I was addicted. However, Rita had a zero-tolerance policy for injection drug use among ranch crew members.

"Listen, hon, if you have yourself a couple of Rainiers (beer), it may quiet down those voices just as good as the needle, ok?"

So, I complied with Rita's treatment program. I can recall the first night I sat around the deck with the crew. Drinking and bullshitting. Hal had the iron trash can we used as a burn-barrel situated in the pit hole at the center of the deck to accommodate a small fire without any risk of burning the deck down. We sat huddled pretty closely around the pit, boots propped up on the burn-barrel. In the twisted world of the jungle encampment, our ranch was the shining house on the hill. We had complete privacy for the most part. Rita had an established policy that business was not conducted on the ranch.

"We ain't gonna shit where we eat, boys."

Rita would collect cash from Donnie around noon each day after he completed his morning rounds. She would count it, hand $60 to each crew member, and then the twins would take the rest of the cash to a safety deposit box located about a mile or two outside the jungle. Rita would make the trip to the deposit box herself about once a week for accounting purposes. Obviously, our matriarch had a lot of trust in all of us. Everyone was more than content with the situation and felt taken care of.

Concerning my mental health issues, the other members of the ranch were incredibly supportive. Rita had spent a lot of time with me talking about how my life would continue to be affected by whispers, not defined by them.

"You are gonna need to keep lookin' for ways push them voices to the back, hon. You gotta know what's real and when that little mind of yours is trying to mess with ya."

The presence of my whispers was becoming less torturous. Rita was on to something with the use of alcohol to self-medicate, along with her version of psychotherapy. I kept a pretty constant buzz going, making it easier to ignore them and allowing them to sink into the background. However, there were still moments every day when I struggled to differentiate the hallucinations from reality. Truth be told, staying busy was most helpful. Having something to work on, some kind of purpose. The ranch provided me with opportunities to participate in a working environment, however twisted it was.

Rita started me off on grocery runs. I'd make a daily trip out of the jungle with Hal to pick up supplies. Mostly food. Pretty soon, I was cooking hot meals over the burn-barrel. We placed cast iron griddles over the grate on top of the barrel. It was nice to have a role within the crew, to feel like I was contributing. I became a pretty good cook, under the instruction of Rita, of course.

As the ranch sat in the jungle, it was on the edge of the encampment, pushed against a hill covered in trees and thick blackberry bushes that were impossible to navigate. It really was a jungle. A machete was required to make even one step into the dense growth. The growth density extended only a hundred yards up a steep grade before running up against a busy city street. The growth and the steep grade acted as a barrier to a different world. This made it so the ranch was unreachable from the outside and guarded like a castle on the hill from the inside. Hal liked to hack around in this shrubbery behind the camp. It reminded him of war or something. He had carved out a path through the growth. It was narrow and a bit difficult to navigate intentionally. We didn't want anyone to wander down the green belt and stumble onto the ranch patio. So, it was hidden, but we had a back door out of the jungle that nobody knew about. This was the path used when the twins left to deposit cash and when Hal and I went on grocery runs. Any time a member of the ranch crew left the jungle, this was our hidden exit. Nobody else could have known about it.

Canto II

As I got to know Rita, she gradually described her experience as the daughter of a schizophrenic father and the mother of a son with schizophrenia. She never declared she had all the answers for me. But she offered her knowledge and wanted to help me deal with the whispers and learn to function at a high level despite the distraction of psychosis.

"How are you feelin' today, hon?"

"Ok, thank you."

"I'm going to have you go through the rounds with Donnie." Rita began to cross-train me to fill in for other crew members. Donnie didn't mind. He was a real pro. Donnie chose to live in the jungle because he was wanted for various crimes, including attempted murder. So, he was living off the grid. Donnie would occasionally take a night off from the ranch to rent a motel room with cash. Rita paid him well, more than the other members. After all, he was the face of the business.

Donnie was a fast-talking ninja, had no problem showing me his beat, not threatened by me at all. He wanted an assistant anyway.

"Just follow along with me and act like you've done it before. All we bout to do is sell drugs to a bunch of junkies. You ain't got no reason to be afraid of these motherfuckers. They would sell their eye-balls for a bag of black tar. They ain't got no guns or no shit like that. If they ever did, they sold it as soon as they ran out of cash and bought a bag from me. If they ever pulled one out, they'd be dead anyway."

As we approached the pallet path that led off the ranch, down the bluff into the heart of the jungle, Donnie gave an obvious nod to Quincy and Clive, who were sitting silently in front of their tents. This non-verbal communication indicated to the twins that Donnie was leaving to complete his daily rounds. We walked down the path and started off on the circular route. After we were a couple hundred yards off the ranch, I looked back to see the twins creeping down the bluff behind us.

Donnie explained the security detail provided by the twins, "Quincy and Clive will flank us on the route. If any shit goes down or anyone gets an attitude, they will fuck somebody up."

Donnie worked quickly. I was able to follow him around and observe, but his communication pace was difficult for me to keep up with when the whispers were chatting in the back of my ear. There were a couple of customers who begged for a comped bag to avoid becoming dope sick. I could empathize with them a bit, thinking back to the last time I was desperate in that way.

However, Donnie had no sympathy for them, "Get your ass a piece of cardboard. The freeway onramp is over there."

I wouldn't say that Donnie was overly-harsh or anything. It just never crossed his mind to provide heroin for free.

As the route continued, a couple of junkies approached Donnie to make a purchase and were scolded for doing so.

"What the fuck you walking up on me for? Are you fucking stupid? You must be."

The twins were suddenly lurking behind the misguided customers. Donnie was not open to being approached by customers for several reasons. Primarily, he didn't want to attract the wrong kind of attention. It was known to the animals in the jungle that Donnie was the source of heroin. But Donnie didn't want to make it obvious to a casual observer, to a cop in street clothes who may wander into the jungle to scope out the joint and sniff around like a weasel in the forest.

The entire route took between two and three hours, starting on the south end, twisting and tunneling through different pockets of the jungle. Needles littered the trail like candy wrappers on a playground. Donnie navigated the layers of the jungle like a tour guide on the safari. The twins stalked in the dark shadows, ready to pounce like lions. The central jungle was the most dangerous. This is where many young refugees camped, having come to America from third-world countries, ending up marginalized back into the same standard of life by the America they longed to be accepted by. They were angry about this, hopeless and desperate. No options at all. They sought relief from their suffering with heroin, as I had in the arboretum.

Tents were not the only variety of living spaces in the jungle. Clever jungle residents would erect plywood walls. Various other materials had been schlepped in from one of America's wealthiest cities whose business district was less than a mile away. Like the ranch crew, some folks live there voluntarily, other than me. Most jungle folks were stuck there because of tragic circumstances, to no fault of their own. Myself, for example, I made a choice. I had decided that going back to my parents was not an option. That decision was void of logic, but I was subject to a certain tunnel vision at the time. I couldn't see the options available beyond my basic needs. I may have been the only schmuck in the jungle who was actively avoiding a life of relative privilege to live in the gutter of American society.

Donnie didn't have much to worry about. Law enforcement didn't *really* give a shit about the jungle. A bunch of junkies camping in the woods? Fuck em. They don't care about that layer of society's underbelly. They just figured a bunch of low-level hustlers were under the freeway, shooting up whenever a scrap of currency fell off the table close enough for the jungle rats to scurry over to it. Throwaways were of no use in even providing a supply of clean needles or a proper disposal bin for them to reduce disease transmission. They figured the rats in the jungle were already lousy with hepatitis and HIV.

Donnie was not a low-level hustler. In fact, the ranch crew was moving a significant amount of product. I continued to follow along with Donnie for the rounds a few days a week, whenever Rita asked me to. The layers of the ranch operation began to peel back, and I could see its complexity. At one point during the daily rounds, Donnie handed me the set of mini-binoculars he carried with him to examine the details in the distance. "Look back at the ranch, just behind Hal's tent up in the bush." There Hal was, propped up in one of the old-growth Evergreens on a hunting stand, rifle at his side, looking right back at me like an eagle. Donnie wanted me to know that he took this operation seriously. He wanted me to focus. But, it was hard for me to keep up with him. First of all, Donnie could talk circles around anyone and then into a corner. A world-class manipulator. His level of intelligence was very advanced.

Moreover, I was trying to function with schizophrenia treated by booze and the counsel of a homeless woman who had a family history of schizophrenia. She wanted to help me to prove something to herself. My services were not needed by Donnie. I was just dragging my paddle through a sea of black tar.

"You may not be useful as a dealer, but it was good experience tagging along with Donnie for a while, hon. I want you to understand what's goin' on here, and you can't learn it all from hearing me yap," Rita explained.

I appreciated the opportunities Rita was providing for me. It was clear she viewed me as a project. Even I could see that. She ended up explaining to me how her father was supported by her mother. Her mother had become pregnant around sixteen, and her father was a couple years older and experienced the onset of schizophrenia around the time of Rita's birth. She characterized her relationship with her father as tragic. He had been put on some powerful anti-psychotic medications in the 1960s that turned him into a slobbering sack of sedated potatoes. He would come off the meds and have a week or two of relatively stable life before winding back down his canyon of psychosis. Then he would get back onto the meds again. That was his pattern. Distress around her father's mental status was a constant in her formative years. This type of distress continued similarly with her own son. Rita seemed to be experiencing the same kind of recurring dynamic in her adulthood that she had in her childhood. Perhaps the fact that she had essentially adopted me into her chosen family was part of her dysfunction. She couldn't help herself when she saw me wander into certain peril that day when I followed those vagrants from downtown along the hidden urban path to this haunted village.

"You remind me of my son when he first started hearing his voices."

Since becoming Donnie's sidekick was not in the cards with me, I spent some time with Hal. He showed me how to repair the patio and tried to teach me how his custom rainwater collection system operated. But Hal preferred to work alone. He enjoyed the company at the ranch, but his daily routine and the tasks he was responsible for were a source of solitude for him. The old vet had been operating that way for so long that he wasn't capable of anything different. So, I continued to make grocery runs and do most of the cooking. We paid a couple of guys from the jungle with methamphetamine to get rid of the trash from the ranch about twice per week. Meth wasn't a drug that we sold a lot of because Rita feared its users due to their severe paranoia and work ethic. She preferred to keep folks pretty sedated. Safer, easier to control. Although the jungle did have its share of coke and meth users, they were active enough to get their substances offsite daily, and usually, they were just passing through like intoxicated ships in the night. As long as they weren't encroaching on the heroin customer base in the jungle, they were no concern to Rita.

Canto III

Occasionally, Rita would have the twins tune someone up to send a message, but typically, it had little to do with business. If Rita became aware of a rape that occurred in the jungle, she would watch the twins beat the guy down to a few brain cells. No hesitation there. She admitted once after several drinks that she had been assaulted by her uncle throughout her childhood. I only heard it mentioned one time. She was not the type to be vulnerable. Rita was our leader, and she never showed any weakness.

As my symptoms leveled off to moderate pitch, like a whisper loop, I could see that keeping myself occupied was the best way to keep the voices at bay. The booze made them easier to tolerate, as mentioned previously. I made runs to the liquor store for the group on a Schwinn with a backpack. Rita just gave me money most of the time, but sometimes the crew members picked up the tab from their share of the take. We had a full bar on the patio of the ranch. It was acceptable to start drinking as soon as the daily sales route was completed and all of my other daily tasks had been accomplished. After a few bizarre incidents, Rita made me stick to beer, during which I got a little too drunk-horny and jerked myself off like a dog with a skin issue. Whiskey-dicked and unable to ejaculate, I jerked off for way too long. Or so I was told. I blacked out every time that happened. The rest of the ranch crew was able to handle their liquor well. They were heavy drinkers but always had enough of their wits about them to guard the ranch from peril.

It didn't happen much, but occasionally, someone from the jungle would decide to pay us a visit. Outsiders were strictly forbidden from setting foot on our campsite or even approaching the bluff that the ranch sat on. Rita was crystal clear about that. Most of the time, when someone approached the ranch, it was a misguided drug seeker. However, there was an incident where two guys raided us intending to take money and drugs. It was around 3 am, and I woke up from the gunshots. Hal saw them coming. He was awake and alert, keeping watch as usual. He could have just told them to fuck off. He didn't want to. Two pops broke up the silence of the night. I'm sure folks scattered around the area heard the noise and knew what made that kind of sound. But many of the heroin users probably slept right through it without coming close to noticing. Those who did hear probably couldn't tell exactly where the shots came from in the dense overgrowth of this wooded urban wasteland.

At any rate, Hal plugged both of them in the side of the head from short range with a very old six-shooter he kept strapped to his ankle. Hal had them wrapped in garbage bags and duct tape almost immediately and dragged them up the hill through the path he had hacked out of the hillside for situations such as this. He buried both of them up there somewhere. After the bodies were out of the campsite, the twins broke down Quincy's tent and ripped apart a section of the patio that blood was splattered on. They started up a fire in the barrel and had everything burned pretty quickly. Nobody seemed to think twice about it. The cost of doing business. Hal replaced the patio section the following day. Quincy needed a new tent anyway.

This incident solidified me within the ranch crew. I had achieved some bona fides. I knew where the bodies were buried. Rita expressed to the group a bit of concern over killing those two jagoffs, "Keep your ear to the ground, boys. If this brings any heat at all, we are gone."

So, we continued operating the same way, the only difference being that Donnie collected the information we were looking for during the daily route. He would know if killing those two guys had put the ranch crew on the radar of law enforcement. Donnie was pretty convincing about his ability to gather information, "I'll talk the tits off a stripper."

The twins' fierce loyalty to Rita was astounding. The consummate stoic soldiers, standing by at all times, looking for an opportunity to provide service to Rita in exchange for her maternal presence, along with an employment opportunity. I mean, Quincy and Clive weren't submitting W2s, but they were receiving payment for their contribution to the business. Any mid-level drug operation needs an enforcer or two, and the ranch had that in spades with Quincy and Clive.

Regarding where the ranch crew was getting the large volume of drugs from, Rita kept her source very close to the vest. She only brought the twins with her to pick up the product. She was able to get it pretty directly, judging by the fact that it came in a brick-like it was handed to her straight from a cartel mule. She'd bring a brick back to the ranch twice a week, and Donnie would chop it up like a Japanese sous chef with a Ginsu knife. He bagged it up and packaged it. In terms of experience in the drug trade, the ranch wasn't Donnie's first rodeo.

Rita was having pretty regular sleepovers with a couple different women from the jungle community. She kept it very casual. Very few women were around the jungle community, but Rita seemed to find the queer women out of the bunch pretty easily. Rita was mostly interested in getting her rocks off, and that's it. She'd order the gals around like beaten dogs. Rita was an angry, controlling, sexist male at her core. Mostly what she wanted to do was count her money and get drunk with the boys. I didn't think of her as a woman despite her birth sex.

Eventually, we started seeing different types of activity in the jungle. New species were moving in. The demand for heroin continued, but the population overall increased and brought a fair amount of amphetamine-addicted criminals. Suddenly a number of shacks began to erect as these guys toted in materials like pack rats with Mexican jumping beans stuffed up their rectums. Strange structures, like burning-man, got lost and forgot how to find his way back to the desert from the rainforest, but with cheaper drugs. Donnie was a bit irritated and concerned about these 'jumping beans', which is how he referred to meth users. The ranch crew was definitely not exerting the level of control in the jungle that Rita was used to. The jumping beans weren't natural enemies of ours. But, they were opportunists and completely unpredictable. They could get a wild hair in their ass and decide to raid the ranch at any moment. We were pretty sure the two guys who'd already tried to raid us were cut from this cloth. We couldn't tell for sure because it was hard to see if their teeth were decayed in that meth-y kind of way due to the gunshot wounds. Hal had plugged them in the face at point-blank range.

Donnie warned, "It's just a matter of time with these motherfuckers. They know I'm holding, and they're coming."

The operation continued as these jumping beans continued to not sleep. They would get focused on weird shit and walk themselves in circles for days.

Meanwhile, I continued to work with Rita on coping with my whispers as she trained me to think of the whispers as a strength somehow. The trick was coming up with their utility.

"Listen, hon, you have a radio playing classical music inside your head, just encouraging you along."

I listened to Rita. She would check in with me a few times a day as she reinforced her approach and walked me through psychosis like a service dog leading its blind owner to a crosswalk.

"Them whispers is just the music of your life, like birds chirping in the morning. You don't need to listen too close. If Michael Jackson tells you to beat it, you don't stop what you're doing and punch a dog." Rita didn't expect me to just snap out of my psychosis like a twisted hypnotist had put a spell on me that needed to be exercised. She brought me along slowly and had an understanding of my illness. I couldn't be talked out of it, but I could improve how I interact with the whispers over time. Even in the distressing environment of the jungle, I had been able to avoid being influenced into a fixed delusion like the river ditch situation. My insight about the illness had improved under Rita's tutelage. I was more aware every day.

It had become a somewhat rare occurrence for me to join Donnie on the rounds at this point. I still tagged along occasionally, but due to the ranch crew's increased concern about the jumping beans, Donnie requested that I stay back at the ranch during rounds. He thought I could provide more of a contribution that way. Hal set me up with a tree stand, and I joined him as a lookout in an effort to increase our security. We also started using walkie-talkies to communicate with the twins as Donnie made his way through the rounds. Hal had me scout for any movement around Donnie. Hal also focused on tracking the twins' movement. He would radio to them any warnings or information he thought would be helpful. It was an efficient operation. As the situation became more and more dangerous due to the unpredictability of the jumping beans, we would get down from the stands and follow the sales team from a distance, scanning with binoculars. If some jumping bean was planning an assault on Donnie and the twins, they'd have some warning from us. Starting out from the tree stands allowed Hal to get a lay of the land, and he would know if anything was odd, an ambush being set up or whatever. We could get the warning out to the sales team right away to get the fuck out of there.

We began running into conflict on the sales route. The jumping beans did not give us the respect we were used to. One day we were on foot trailing the sales team on the North Side. This was maybe a week into the new security detail. We crossed paths with a small group of guys we hadn't seen before. One of them was the clear alpha with a douchy sidekick. The other two seemed to be mostly along for the ride. Hal radioed ahead to the twins and alerted them. These guys appeared to be passing through. They were predators thinking they could pick off prey from the herds of heroin addicts in the jungle, looking to jump someone for pleasure. These were evil fuckers. They could see the way Donnie carried himself, his swagger, and that pissed them off. They were disgusting as they approached Donnie, "Hey nigger, get over here. I have a question to ask you." A couple of hyenas who just wandered into the lion's den with a tremendous display of ignorance. The section of the jungle where this encounter occurred was densely populated. In other words, many folks heard what that guy said and knew who he had said it to. The level of disrespect was obviously going to require some retribution. I could see in Donnie's eyes that he was seeing red.

"I got a nigga for you, boy." Quincy and Clive were good enough at their jobs that these two white-trash jumping beans had no indication they were associated with Donnie at all. Probably didn't even notice them. Clive approached the guy who made the statement from behind, who was now wielding a knife along with his buddy. Clive struck him with a baton he kept in his backpack along with a number of other 'work-related' tools. The strike was delivered with the accuracy of an orthopedic surgeon, right where the spine meets the skull. Dropped him like a sack of potatoes. The second guy quickly realized that he was fucked and tried to give himself a chance by running. However, Quincy was on him like a lion dragging a weak zebra to the ground. A public display of power followed. Anyone unaware that the twins were king in this jungle had been put on red alert. Rita's strongmen had once again shown their metal. The two of them were beaten within a breath or two from death. Donnie and Clive had corralled the other two members of the group who hadn't exactly known what they were getting themselves into as they went along with the plan of their now brain-damaged buddies. The two of them stood trembling, hands raised over their heads, faces pointed down as their body language communicated submission. Donnie hollered orders at them like a livid drill sergeant compensating for an abusive drunken father.

"Pick these mothafuckers up or drag em. I don't give a fuck how. Get them out of here now! If I see a cop come through asking any questions about this beating, I'm going to find you, and you gonna get it till you dead squealing like the stuck ass pigs that you are." Clive and Quincy padded them down as Donnie issued the order, removed their wallets, and handed them to Donnie. The active commentary was provided as he mined through their wallets, stating out loud their full names, addresses and pulling out a photograph from one of the wallets of a female toddler.

"One cop or just any indication, and we will kill you in your sleep. I am going to keep this picture. Go on and get!" Donnie also kept their Washington State Drivers licenses. Those two guys were going to be paranoid for the rest of their lives due to the fear that Donnie placed on their souls that day. The other two guys wouldn't be talking any time soon, and if they did regain the ability to verbally communicate, it wouldn't be making much sense. We weren't very concerned about any blowback that this very public display could bring to the ranch in the form of law enforcement. This incident was viewed as an opportunity to demonstrate our authority, and we took advantage of it. They did, at least, but I was there with a tough look on my face.

Canto IV

As you can imagine, the sales route had become burdensome on the morale of the crew due to the increasingly combative environment in the jungle. However, luckily, I was not feeling the heat like the rest of the crew. For me, it was less dangerous. I wasn't asked to engage in any violent conflict, and Rita wouldn't allow me to carry a firearm. So, basically, I was just a lookout. I would follow the group as we spanned out on the route like a group of geese in formation.

Then all of a sudden, Maggie appeared like a ghost entering back into the living world as I stood against an evergreen with a pair of binoculars looking like a voyeur with a very specific fetish.

"Hey, Jack! What the fuck, man? What's going on?"

"Maggie!? Jesus, what the fuck are you... Look, I can't talk now," I said as emotion flooded throughout my body.

Hal shot me a glare from his position a hundred yards away.

"Meet me back at this spot at 2 pm," she said and vanished.

We continued the sales route. I was buzzing on the thought of Maggie, but I needed to continue following the twins through the layers of hell. I was about a hundred yards away from where I had run into Maggie as I got pulled back by another familiar voice. It was Alvin, the vociferous drug salesman I had met in jail.

"Yo, Jack! I thought that was you. So, you know Maggie too? She was a customer of mine until recently, she's clean now, but she's a good friend, so I support that. I just saw you talking with her. I'm in the same camp. She told me there would be a good market for my products here." As Alvin was saying that, he began to feel the presence of the twins moving into his space.

"What's up, brotha?" Alvin reached out his hand to Quincy gregariously. It was not reciprocated.

"It's good to see you, Alvin. But you should know that the jungle territory is spoken for," I was direct with Alvin. No need to have him learn it the hard way.

"I can see that, Jack. I got it. I'm out. You won't see me in here again. But, hey, Maggie has been looking for you, man. She's a good girl. I haven't fucked with her or anything."

"Thanks, Alvin, I appreciate that. I gotta check in with my boss." At that point, I could feel the twins' breath on my back. I needed to end the conversation. I quickly shook hands with Alvin, and we moved on.

It was actually a relief to know Maggie had been running in the same crew with Alvin. He may have been a drug pusher, but he was no predator. A drug salesman with a heart of gold. All of that happened so fast I was still trying to get my thoughts straight. It seemed my world had been turned upside down once again. I needed to see Maggie.

Back at the ranch, I informed Rita I would meet with a former girlfriend I knew from the arboretum.

"Good for you, hon. You didn't tell me you had a girlfriend over there."

I described to Rita the brief but intimate relationship Maggie, and I had for about a month or so, hoping that Rita would approve. After all, Rita was firmly in control of my basic needs, not to mention that she was also my most trusted alley and lifeline. I desperately wanted Rita to allow me to bring Maggie into the ranch to stay with me. I was certain they would love each other.

"Go ahead, hon. But, I'm gon' have the twins tail you, just this time. We may be a target right now. But, we ain't gonna be no easy target."

A suspicious approach from Rita was to be expected. She didn't know who I was going to meet, and she wanted to protect me, along with her business. When she mentioned a target, she was thinking that *I* would be an easy one. So, I didn't blame her at all for the concern. Why wouldn't I want to have the twins rolling with me through the jungle? I would feel safer with them around me, guarding me like two vicious dogs. I could have pulled my dick out and pissed on someone if I wanted to in their presence, and nobody would fuck with me. Plus, Maggie would see that I was a part of something real. Not just a bunch of junkies sleeping on top of each other.

I would now be meeting Maggie without the heroin mindset and was anxious about how that would go. Alvin had said she was clean too. I wondered if our relationship could work without it. My life was a roller coaster. I had morphed into a different person several times over the past several months. Most likely, what I had with Maggie was a flash in the pan. Situationally, we were sort of limited within the pool of mates. But, we did have a strong connection, and her support and Rita's might combine to make me something normal.

Walking through the jungle with the twins at this point was a satisfying exercise. Their authority was impressive. The body language we received from the residents of the jungle embodied appeasement. Hat in hand, looking at the ground kind of thing. Never in my life have I felt more like royalty than I did that day strolling through the jungle with Quincy and Clive as my bodyguards. I could feel the desire dripping through their veins, looking for an opportunity for violence. The only thing keeping these guys from murdering the entire village was Rita's structure provided to them. She had an almost artful command of Quincy and Clive. If not for Rita, they would have been locked up long ago for giving in to their uncontrolled desire to take life.

I'd been dealing with so many emotions and hopeful thoughts since running into Maggie that I'd hardly noticed the whispers, reinforcing the idea that Rita had been trying to wire into my thought process: living a busy, normal life quiets the voices. Things that I give a shit about have always been the most effective distraction. At this moment, I was again infatuated with Maggie. And there she was, like a regal lioness gracing us with her presence.

"Who are these guys?" It was a natural question to ask, but Maggie was a natural, so it was also fitting.

"Maggie, this is Quincy, and here is Clive. These are my friends. They watch out for me sometimes. Our boss doesn't want me out on my own too much." The twins started getting uncomfortable, shushing me in their secret way as I said that. I was being told not to share any more information, especially not about 'our boss'. They may have felt a kinship toward me as a ranch member, but ultimately they were loyal to Rita. They didn't want Maggie to know what we were.

"They don't need to stay with us. Let's just go to your campsite. They will watch from a distance but don't need to be on top of us. Sorry about that, didn't mean to put you off," I tried to assure her.

"It's fine. I'm just confused. Why do you have bodyguards?"

"Look," I said, "let's not focus on that."

She didn't want to take me to her site because she didn't want to scare her community with the presence of the twins. So, Maggie and I found a spot to plop down, and the twins stepped into the background where they had themselves a dip of Copenhagen, waiting silently. Maggie hugged me, and it felt great. It had been a number of months since I'd last experienced the grace of her affection. She seemed well.

"Jack, you look good, like you haven't been injecting for a while."

"Same goes for you."

"I started taking methadone. I have to walk over to this clinic every day to take it because they won't let you have any extra doses. But I don't crave heroin that much."

I didn't know what methadone was, but Maggie went on about how it's meant as replacement therapy for heroin, like nicotine gum for smokers.

"I haven't injected for a couple months or so. The folks I stay with made it a condition of my residence at our campsite," I informed her of my own sobriety.

"How are you dealing with your voices? Did you start taking meds?"

"No. I've been working every day with someone on coping with them. I mainly stay really busy, and it distracts me enough not to obsess over them. Plus, I drink a lot of beer which numbs them out a bit." Maggie nodded along, understanding my situation. I had missed her gracious body language.

"I got released from jail real quick, and I was put into the drug court since I'd been through the jail a few times after getting picked up with heroin," she said. "They're the ones who got me into the methadone program."

"Where have you been staying?" I hadn't seen her around the jungle, so she couldn't have been here for long. I'd been on surveillance with the ranch crew since the heat was cranked up a few weeks earlier, and I would have noticed if she had been near.

"I went back to stay with an old foster parent for a bit. But he's a nasty old man, and I'd rather sleep in the slum than have to suck his dick for rent."

"Are you protected at your campsite? There are a lot of dirtbags around here, and you are the only attractive woman I've seen in the jungle since I stumbled in." Maggie was visibly smitten with the compliment.

"I don't know. Where do you camp? Can I stay with you?"

My heart felt like it had melted into my intestines when she said that.

I couldn't lie to Maggie and tell her how she would be welcome to join me on the ranch. It was going to be a tall order to get Rita to agree to let her step foot onto the deck, let alone sleep there. Rita was paranoid like a mob boss. The thing was, Rita had no way of vetting Maggie. The jungle was more anonymous than the dark web. I consulted the twins about this matter on the way back. They had no feedback to offer in terms of an effective approach to getting Rita to allow Maggie onto the ranch. In fact, they had no feedback at all other than side-mouth chuckles. But I could tell that Quincy and Clive were rooting for me on this one.

I had trouble sifting through the whispers as I thought about what I would say to Rita. This helped me realize that my most convincing case would be made with the angle that most closely represented the truth: I thought that Maggie's presence would help me to Rita had given me the tools, and Maggie gave me the support. Of course, my thought process was a bit misguided. But I was sure that I had a compelling case to present to Rita.

I framed the idea of Maggie moving into my tent as if it came from Rita's guidance on how to cope with the whispers effectively, "Maggie will help me focus on real life. She knows what I'm going through. She's been around this stuff a lot. It would allow me to focus on her and turn the volume down in my head," I pleaded.

"I see what you did there, hon. And I appreciate your approach. Tell you what, I want the best for you, but we gotta make sure that Miss Maggie ain't danger to the crew or the business."

"Okay, how do you do that?"

Ain't directions for how to do that, hon. I'm gonna need to talk to her at least. But, first, I'm gonna have the boys watch her for a couple of days to see who she's got buzzing around her. Does she have a group she stays with? A young girl like that must have some kind of protection in a place like this."

"Yeah, she's staying with a group of folks. One guy I know from jail, his name is Alvin, and he's trustworthy. She didn't want me bringing the twins to her site because it would scare the shit out of everyone."

"Sounds like she has a little sense about her. You said you met her in the arboretum. We can't have no junkies around us at all. You know that."

"She's clean, doing a methadone program. She has to go there every day."

"Well, we gotta make sure she can keep her mouth shut on top of everything. We could use a cook anyway, especially since we are all spending so much more time on the route since the jumping beans started pouring in here with meth."

"What should I tell her?"

"Let her know that I'll go with you tomorrow to visit her. I'll put Hal on her ass tonight, and we'll see if she's got any filth stuck to her that won't shake off easy."

So, I walked back to where I met with Maggie earlier in the day, the twins and Hal followed. I told her I would have to meet back with her the next day at the same time. The twins and I returned to the ranch. Hal was already blended into the scenery. We'd see him tomorrow for his report. I was hopeful that Maggie would clear his surveillance review, but I didn't know what she was up to. Maybe she was just fishing for a better option? I hoped that her intentions were pure like China white. But in reality, she was more of an Afghani-black-tar kind of girl. The life I'd been indoctrinated into over the previous months had made me into a skeptic.

Rita, Quincy, Clive, and I hung out on the deck drinking that night while Hal collected information on Maggie's potential risk to the crew. As we did most nights, Rita and I spent a good amount of time discussing how the whispers presented themselves in my mind during the day and how I could work around them. As usual, I felt empowered by Rita. I wasn't surprised that she was open to having Maggie stay with us despite the significant risk she could bring to the crew. Rita was committed to helping me achieve a life of relative normalcy, which she could not do for her son. Her commitment to facilitating my recovery was some sort of compensation for her inability to meet her son's needs long ago, it seemed. Something was motivating her to support me, and it wasn't my contribution to the ranch crew, which was minimal at best.

We hit the sack with a healthy buzz as the twins pissed away the barrel fire that night. I laid down, listening to the whispers speak softly to my intoxicated brain, thinking of how pleasant it would be to enjoy Maggie's company. I awoke the next morning and grabbed a water bottle to wet my beak and pour it over my head. The twins had already gone on a supply run and returned with hiker packs full of canned food and water. Those bastards never had a hangover in their otherwise traumatic lives. Hal wandered back in, and we all had something to eat.

Hal tried his best to cut through the fog, "Well, it just looks like a bunch of strung-out junkies. We deliver to those little buggers all the time. Donnie can probably tell you about the cut of their job."

"Anything that concerns you?" Rita asked with an irritated tone. She wasn't satisfied with Hal's report.

"Depends. No jumping beans creeping around her or anything. I didn't see anyone I would be worried about as a threat to the crew. I wouldn't even give em that much credit. Basically, just an average group of jungle-junkies. Three tents. She stayed in one by herself. No visitors. Looks like she just started camping around here."

"Why is that?" Rita was short again.

"Well, from the looks of her, she should have a bunch of rapists creeping up to her tent, trying to get a piece of her ass. So, I don't think she's been here long because she hasn't turned up on the offender types radar yet. And she doesn't appear to be anyone's property, no protection. She's just out here on her own. Only a matter of time until something pretty bad happens to that little darling."

Suddenly, Rita seemed a bit more satisfied. Perhaps she needed Hal to say Maggie was vulnerable and non-threatening. Or maybe she just wanted to know that she's attractive.

"Okay. Mr. Jack and I will visit her. Jack, if I look her in the eye and see that opiate droop, she ain't gonna be coming round here at all."

"Of course, Rita."

As I walked through the jungle with Rita, the twins in tow, it was clear that she was known among the residents even though she didn't show her face in the public arena very often. The way she carried herself, the quiet confidence. She wore cowboy boots and openly carried as if to inform the peasants that the sheriff is in town, be on your best behavior. Nobody else in the crew was allowed to open carry, concealed only. But nobody told Rita what to do. She made the rules. She would provide consequences when necessary. The twins were on high alert. Their hypervigilance reached a fever pitch when they were escorting Rita. Like secret servicemen escorting Obama through an NRA convention.

We showed up earlier than Maggie. Rita was predictably unpredictable. As we approached her tent, I called out for her, "Maggie, you there? It's me, Jack."

"Hey, I'm over here."

There she was, in all her seductive glory. She emerged from the overgrowth, a coy smile on her face, "I'm just getting back from the methadone clinic."

Rita took charge. "How ya doin, darling, my name is Reee-tah," she said with phonemic authority, "and these are my associates," a casual hand wave to indicate Hal and the twins were with *her* and not the other way around. Donnie was not present. Rita didn't want to stir up any anxiety amongst the customer base. "Jack asked me if you could come stay in my camp. I thought that was sweet. So sweet, in fact, that it made me curious... Why do you want to stay with a bunch of roughnecks like us, sweetheart?"

"Well, Jack and I stayed together a few months back, and I fell in love with him." Rita prompted her to continue with a curious nod. "I just want to be with him, ma'am," Maggie nodded to Rita with that graceful, understanding body language of her own that was so hypnotizing, "I'll do whatever you tell me. I don't have anyone or anything. I mean you no harm. I am trying to get connected to Jack again because I love him. And yes, I am desperate in other ways. I don't have anywhere to go. I've been trying to find a place to be my entire life." This moment erupted with the kind of emotion that my psychosis had inhibited for several months.

"Can you cook over an open fire?" Rita was already gauging Maggie's utility.

"Yes, ma'am, I have been homeless a lot, lived outside a lot. Usually as the only female in the camp." Rita was sold with that angle, perfectly executed by Maggie. The female plight in a lawless man's world was a subject Rita had contemplated throughout her rough-and-tumble life. Maggie, unintentionally, made a permanent connection to Rita at that moment. She appealed to the slice of Rita's brain that was committed to altruism. It was a small slice, but potent.

Rita contained her smitten emotion with crafty personality talent. "Oh, one more thing, my dear, I'm gonna need to take a close look at you when we get back to the ranch. Need to check you for needle marks."

"Well, I was a heroin addict up until two weeks back, so you *will* find that."

"Couple weeks, eh? I'll be able to tell if they are more recent than that, dear. See you at the ranch." Rita turned and walked away as she wrapped the meeting. She was off. Clive and Quincy peeled off and splayed behind her like good soldiers.

"Jack, what's the ranch?" Maggie asked.

If only I could summarize.

Canto V

I understood at this point that Maggie was a tool in Rita's project to fix me. She wanted me to have someone, a companion. But I struggled to determine how I would explain the situation to Maggie. She would see that we ran a heroin sales operation in the jungle. Like shooting junkies in a barrel. What would she think of that? It wasn't my role to explain the business to Maggie. I just helped her get settled in. Of course, it was surreal to find myself cohabitating with her once again. Albeit strangely different because we were no longer heroin junkies. But that shouldn't matter, right? We were in love before, as junkies, our love should be sturdy enough to hold up against sobriety, right?

To each is their own kind of thing. It felt different, but we were giving it a shot. It was all about appeasing Rita anyway. We both felt pressure from her to be what she wanted. Rita had been so benevolent toward me. First, she saved my life by bringing me in when I was on death's door, wandering into the jungle like the zombie apocalypse had arrived. I finally felt like I was in a situation where I could enjoy my life, not only survive.

"Come on over, dear," Rita summoned Maggie to her tent shortly after she stepped foot onto the deck of the ranch, "just need to give you a quick once over, won't take long."

I could only imagine that Rita was going to cop a little bit of a feel, or at least jill herself off later to the mental images of Maggie's bareness, the horny old dike. No matter, Maggie was there to be with me, and I was lucky that Rita was allowing me to have a companion so beggars can't choose.

"Wow, she's a bit grabby," Maggie explained when we got a moment of privacy.

"Are you okay?" I was now worried that Maggie wouldn't stay because Rita had molested her or something.

"Yeah, it's fine. It was nothing, really. She may have cupped my boob a little and examined my nipples a bit thoroughly. Do people inject into their nipples? Anyway, I don't care, she's a nice lady, and I'm just happy to be here, Jack. Maybe she'll get herself off later thinking about me. I don't care."

"Huh, that's what I was thinking too. She's probably twiddling herself right now." We shared a laugh and then an awkward silence, probably due to my nerves.

"*I* want to be doing the twiddling," I blurted out boldly.

"Jack, can I kiss you?"

We melted into each other, her touch tender. I could tell that we were both a lot healthier than when we had been together. Her lips were moist, her skin was soft, and her vagina dripped like a slip-and-slide at a porn convention with the odor of passionate secretion. I was so hard I knew it wouldn't last long. The only clothes that came off were our jeans. It was such a mad scramble for indulgence that we took the most direct path to penetration. She grabbed my cock and guided it in like a pipe fitter. It was the perfect combination of hot and wet in there. The feeling of her pulsating so tightly around me was too much. I lasted for maybe three or four thrusts before I burst. Maggie simultaneously reached a climax as well. A moment that provided the best high of my life, a dragon worth chasing. I popped like a water balloon full of warm mayonnaise. It was the first time I'd failed to consider pulling out over my sexual career. The moment had taken over, and it was a different type of release, stronger than one could imagine. I still wonder if psychosis contributed to the perceived power behind that ejaculation. I thought I'd given myself a hernia, but it turned out to be a strained pelvic wall. Maggie was gasping and trembling in a way that was validating to my manhood.

We both fell asleep for a nap as I listened to the whispers serenade me. My brain was bursting with endorphins, the mood so positive that the whispers followed. It was great to be back with Maggie. When we stepped out of the tent an hour later, the rest of the crew sat around the fire on the deck, roasting brats and drinking beer.

"Yall sounded like a couple drunken chimps who just got released to the wild in there," Rita joked as the rest of the crew chuckled in a good-natured kind of way.

It was just harmless ribbing. Maggie knew that Rita was now an ally of hers and her new boss. We had another great night sitting around drinking and smoking cigarettes. Hal shared a story about his long-lost love, a rare moment of vulnerability for him. Quincy and Clive shared their approach to getting laid in brief statements about how they were only interested in casual encounters or, as they put it, "just wanna fuck a bitch and leave yo." Donnie was briefly present before leaving the ranch to actually get laid. He let the Twins know about his sexual exploits and even offered to bring them along, as he often did, which they always declined, "we don't need yo help, Donnie." They did. Too bad because Donnie's silver tongue could have talked a high-end prostitute into getting with the Twins as a training exercise. At any rate, it was a real love-fest. Everyone was happy for Maggie and me. It felt a little like a charity project because of the amount of praise we were getting. I just couldn't tell if it was all authentic or if they were making us feel good because that's what Rita wanted them to do.

The whispers were hushing in the background, but they continued to work with the endorphins blasting through my cranium. Rita and Maggie discussed strategies on how best to support me, and I couldn't help but think how lucky I had always been to be surrounded by the people who loved me so much. My parents' love crossed my mind, and a tear welled up in my eye as it hit me. They were probably worried sick about my well-being. So, I got really drunk and passed the fuck out in an effort to avoid thinking of my folks.

I woke up the next day in a pool of my own piss, which occasionally happened to me when I got drunk out of my mind. A rocky morning ensued as Maggie was forced to deal with my incontinence.

"Does this happen a lot now?"

"No. Sometimes. I'm sorry." I was really fucking hungover.

Maggie gracefully cleaned out the tent and enlisted a bit of help from Hal, who sprayed it out with a makeshift hose that drew water from a jug. It was humiliating. I sat there in my urine-soaked clothes like a fucking buffoon. I had no other option. Maggie definitely seemed a bit concerned. Perhaps some buyer's remorse. I needed to explain what had happened. I needed to tell her how I'd become emotional after the thought of my parents' suffering crossed my mind. But, I didn't want to appear weaker or more flawed. I just kind of withdrew and sulked in my own despair for an hour or so. Rita pushed me along,

"Okay, Jackie, time to get over yourself. I need you on point. Donnie is ready to conduct business. So, get your shit together. Maggie, you just hang around and look pretty darling."

If Rita was the queen of the jungle, Maggie was now starting to look like a princess. I followed the twins down the bluff into the shadows to monitor the activity around the sales team. I scanned, letting my eyes follow anyone who appeared to be a potential threat as usual. Then I saw him. Suspicious as he was creepy, walking with that familiar strut. *It was Tex.*

He must have just started staying in the jungle, or I would have seen him on the sales route I scoured every day. Fucking disgusting bastard, I could see him preying on a vulnerable young man who appeared to be living with a significant mental illness, like me. I couldn't believe it. I wanted to go straight back to the ranch to let Maggie know. I wanted to unleash the wrath of the Twins on this rapist. Given their particular disgust for rapists, they would kill him without a second thought. I was excited, and my heart was racing. I needed to consult Maggie and Rita. I sucked it up and finished the sales route with the rest of the crew. We all matriculated back to the ranch.

Maggie was sitting on the deck with Rita, and they had a bunch of clothes strung up that I'd pissed on earlier. The anxiety of this moment had the whispers turning into stern voices. So, I wanted to consult Rita immediately.

"Hey, I need to talk to you guys."

"What's wrong there, Jackie?" Rita could see the despair right away.

"Maggie, I saw Tex. I think he's staying here now."

"What? Are you sure?"

"Yes, what should we do?" Now, something to keep in mind is that Rita was not aware of Tex or our experience with him. In all my conversations and the work that I had done with Rita, I had not disclosed my interaction with this monster to her. I just wanted to move on from the arboretum.

"Hold on just a sec here, hon. You seem pretty alarmed. What's the deal with this Tex character? Maggie, you can speak up now." Obviously, we needed to be honest with Rita.

"He ran our campsite at the arboretum. He raped me many times, probably raped Jack as well after he injected him with a couple of grams of heroin. That's what he does. He gets young kids to stay at his site, gets them on heroin, and has his way." Rita's brow furrowed. I could see her blood start to boil under that leather skin of hers.

"Well, Jackie, I'm a little bit hurt. I thought you would have told me about this shitty little bastard you call Tex."

"I'm sorry, I just wanted to forget about him."

117

"I'm sure you did. It's okay, hon. Now, we actually have a big problem. I can't let this little shit live, and y'all know that. I'd like to kill him with my own hands. However, I tend to keep em clean these days. The twins, on the other hand, when they catch wind of a rapist like this in the jungle, he is dead as ground beef in a slaughterhouse. And they will want to beat him to death."

Maggie piped in, "Honestly, Rita, he deserves to die. Take him off this earth before he does this to anyone else!" I was a bit shocked by Maggie's aggressiveness.

"Jackie, do you agree with that sentiment?"

"I do."

"Well, can y'all give me just a bit more details before I place an order to have his life ended?"

Maggie and I went on to describe his approach, how he'd engaged both of us the same way, injected us with heroin, and proceeded to rape. It was unmistakable. He had a playbook, and he executed it very effectively. On top of that, Tex worked independently. He wasn't associated with a crew that might come after us for retribution. He was a loner disguised as a leader. This made it an easy decision for Rita, who called together Donnie and Hal to consult before alerting the twins of the issue.

Donnie was very measured in his line of questioning, "Jack, let's be real clear right here, you gotta be sure about this. Once we decide to do this thing, and I'm not saying we shouldn't, Quincy and Clive will become aware. After the twins know, it's over for that dude, way past the point of no return."

"I know it was him, Donnie. It's not the whispers telling me."

Rita gave Hal the floor for a moment, and he made a wise suggestion, "Let's do what we always do: scout it out and make sure. Rita, you can take Maggie. We will leave the twins back on the ranch while we confirm the identity." Rita was in favor. Donne and Hal were doing their jobs as her lieutenants, protecting her.

Rita provided more of a long view, "This move will be our last on the ranch, y'all know that, right?"

"What do you mean?" I hadn't thought it through yet.

"Hon, the heat has been cranking up around here with all these jumping beans creeping around. We've had a good run here, but our lease on this customer base may have already expired. We knew all along this ain't a permanent thing. So, if we take out this little rapist, which we will if you can both confirm it's the guy, we WILL need to move on, lay low for a bit."

Hal and Donnie started gathering some of their things, packing their bags quickly. It became clear that with all of the issues we'd been having with the paranoid meth-heads who had flooded into the jungle over the previous month or so and the dangers they posed to the ranch crew, the polished members of the crew understood that our residency here was going to end. We had one last issue to take care of, which would crank the heat to a level that was not safe for us to stay. If the twins were going to be cut loose on Tex, it would bring a storm of unwanted attention, and cops would be sniffing around the jungle in a short amount of time.

"Okay, I'll tell the twins to hold down the fort. Quincy! Clive!" The twins emerged from their tents and mosied over to the other side of the deck, where we had been huddled up with hushed tones. Rita informed them that we were taking a walk to look for Maggie's brother, and we needed them to stay back for ranch security purposes. They were agreeable. The sales route had been completed for the day, so Rita told them to go ahead and pop a beer or whatever and that we wouldn't be long.

I led the group back to the central area within the jungle, and we waited. Uncharacteristically, we were grouped together, just standing under a tree.

"Can we draw any more attention to ourselves here?" Rita pointed out the obvious.

Hal reasoned, "We could break into two groups and separate Jack from Maggie to see if they both identify the same guy."

Rita affirmed, "Maggie stay with me. Hal, you go off with Jack, Donnie just blend off somewhere and scout separately."

We had the walkie-talkies with us, and Hal led me off to a perch in the woods. Donnie was nowhere to be seen from where we were scouting, but we knew he was tucked into the dense overgrowth nearby. We sat there for about an hour, waiting until Tex crawled out of his rat hole.

"That's him! Skinny white guy with the red hat."

Hal radioed to Rita, "We got a visual." Rita responded to Hal right away and advised him to walk out of earshot from me, "Right back, Jack." I waited for him to come back and fetch me. A few minutes later, he circled back and confirmed that Maggie had also identified Tex as the same guy in the red hat.

"Okay. Let's go, Jack, time to plan the next step." I took this to mean that we had all the confirmation needed. We grouped back together as we walked to the ranch. Maggie had tears in her eyes. Rita had fire in hers.

Donnie assessed the situation, "Looks like I need to finish packing that bag." We were no longer walking with the same level of secrecy. We were about to make a grand exit from the jungle.

"Not much gets past you, Donnie. Everybody needs to get a bag together, one bag. The bulk of our shit stays here cause we are going to be traveling light for a bit of time," Rita directed.

Maggie didn't have anything to say. She seemed to be reliving the trauma she had been subjected to at the hand of Tex. When we returned to the Ranch deck, the twins were there starting a barrel fire, crushing beer as they often did. They hardly gave the group a second look, no questions asked about our very atypical jaunt through the jungle.

"Hey, boys." Rita strutted toward them like John Wayne. "I got a little project for ya. Seems like we have a serial rapist residing in the jungle. In fact, this guy stuck Maggie with heroin and raped her a number of times when she was over in the arboretum with Jackie. Sounds like he must have gotten a bunch of little sugars onto the tar and had his way with them. What do you boys think of that?"

Quincy and Clive erupted simultaneously from the camping chairs they had been sitting in, throwing the chairs backward from the force of their movement.

"I'm gonna cut you boys loose on this rat. It's gonna happen right now, and then we will head straight back here to the ranch and walk right up Hal's secret trail, empty our cash from the safety deposit boxes, then we gone, boys." The twins looked like angry pit bulls after a piece of flesh.

"Where's the rat?" Quincy and Clive asked in unison.

"I'll show you where," Rita explained as she clearly enjoyed the control she possessed over the twins, holding a raw T-bone in front of them and making them beg.

Canto VI

Hal and Donnie were loading their primary firearms. The safeties were off at this point. Their plan was not to fire any shots, but this would be a very unpredictable situation. They were certainly planning to pull the guns for intimidation and compliance purposes.

"Maggie, Jackie, you have the option of watching this, but you need to decide right now." Of course, we wanted to see that piece of shit get beaten to a bloody pulp.

Maggie questioned, "Do I get to say anything to him?"

"Of course, dear. Quincy, Clive, after you have this boy handled, stop for a bit. Maggie wants to get a word in," Rita directed. "Maggie, you go ahead and feel free to spit at him or whatever you want, my dear. Off we go then. Let's leave this shithole with a bang."

The twins were practically skipping their way down the bluff. We went off the ranch and into the jungle for perhaps the final time. Rita marched the twins right through the center of the jungle, the ranch crew on full display. We weren't splayed off, disguising ourselves like we typically would on the sales route. Hal and Donnie seemed excited on a couple of levels: they obviously took joy in seeing the twins get an opportunity to kill, which they needed from time to time. But also for the prospect of leaving the jungle. These guys had been working this business here for about eight months by that time, hoarded a good amount of cash, and they were ready to get the fuck out.

Hal, Donnie, and Rita walked with exposed firearms on their waistlines, with no reason to conceal them. We were about to execute Tex by beating in what would be a very public display. Something of a modern-day public stoning.

Rita pointed out the small tent Tex was staying in as we approached. Clive whipped a switch-blade out and sliced the tent's broadside to expose Tex laying there alone. Probably in his refractory period after a drug-induced rape of some poor soul.

"What the fuck!" Tex screamed in anger but immediately began pleading when he looked into the darkness of Clive's eyes. I positioned myself to view the action and made glancing eye contact with Tex.

"Jack?" Tex was desperately reaching for an ally at this point. "Wait, man! You've got the wrong guy. I don't know you. I just got here!"

The twins turned back at the crew as we stood back with a final look to confirm that this was the guy. Tex had already exposed himself by stating my name.

"That's the one, boys," Rita provided the final verdict as she wielded her significant power over the twins' ability to take life. Tex was dead-to-rights, and he deserved to die a painful death. Quincy smacked the red hat off his head, catching a piece of his face, and proceeded to snatch him by his ratty hair, then drag him out of the tent, squealing like a pig who was set for slaughter. He pulled him into the open with a vice grip on his hair as Tex clenched around his wrists to relieve what was just a taste of the pain to come. Now everyone began to creep out of the dark corners of the overgrowth to see what they had already begun to hear.

They could have kicked his head in and finished him off quickly, but they conservatively reigned down blows to his face and head, taking turns as if they were sharing a toy.

"Hold up, boys. Maggie, how bout you get the last word in on this wasted life."

Maggie was no longer frozen with fear as she approached Tex with vengeful disgust. She was clearly happy to see him get what he had coming.

"You raped me. I don't know how many times! Many others too. I see you now, I see what you are, and your life ends in front of us today." She spat in his face and gave him a swift kick in the nuts for good measure. He was still conscious but not capable of verbal communication at this point as he was held up by Clive, who had snot bubbling from his nose like a rabid dog.

The twins proceeded to pummel him as we knew they would. "Don't get his blood all over your hands now, boys," Rita warned as Tex was now just a piece of flesh dripping all over the grass he lay upon, "he at least has hepatitis." Quincy stomped on his shins and snapped both of his tibialis just to make him suffer, even though he was about to end the man's life. It sounded like a wooden baseball bat wrapped in a towel snapping with a sharp thud.

Clive stomped his head in, and just like that, it was over. Tex's life was over, our time in the Jungle was over, and the clock was ticking on us. Birds chirped as the jungle residents went silent with shock. Due to the public viewing of this murder, it was probably just a matter of time until one of the jumping beans, who had watched from the metaphorical bleachers during this spectacular display of violence, called it in. We hustled back down to the south end of the jungle and back up the bluff onto the ranch for the last time, guns drawn along the way to inform any onlookers that if they got in our way, they would be shot down with no regard for their life.

The animal kingdom of humanity that was the jungle gave us a very wide berth as we passed through for the final time. The twins got hosed down by Hal, had a quick change of clothes, tossed their bloody boots in the barrel, and put on some old county jail sandals. The twisted satisfaction in their eyes was both troubling and exhilarating. A few basic duffle bags sat on the deck, which were swooped up. We scurried up to the secret path that Hal bushwhacked into the overgrowth and frantically climbed through the thick urban forest, grabbing branches and roots to lift ourselves up the steep, muddy hill. We navigated past the spot where Hal buried the two jumping beans who tried to rob us. We leaked out of the back of the forest, ran underneath an overpass, and hopped over a guard rail to reach the city street. Then boarded a city bus just minutes after the murder had occurred. This was the same bus route we often took to get to the grocery store where we purchased our supplies, located right next to the post office Rita had been using to store our cash in safety deposit boxes. As soon as we sat down on the metro bus, Rita pulled out a GoPhone from her backpack, attached a fresh battery to it, and placed a call.

"Hey, it's me. The jig is finally up, and we are headed to clean out the boxes. How quickly can you meet us there?"

I had no idea who she was speaking with. We hopped off the bus, and Rita directed the crew to stay put outside the post office. She brought Hal inside with her, and within two minutes, they were back out, and a Winnebago pulled up. Whoever Rita had called from the bus had a quick response time. It wasn't surprising that Rita had a well-developed escape plan. I'm not sure if the safety deposit boxes were under a false name, but Rita never had any issue accessing those to store our earnings. A large Caucasian male stepped out of the Winnebago.

"Okay, boys, this here is Rick," Rita announced. "He is loaning us his rig so we can go ahead and get out of Dodge City while things cool down around here. So hop on in, and let's get out of Seattle before the little piggies come lookin'. Thanks, Rickie."

We all jumped in the Winnebago with a huge sense of relief along with a feeling of luxury. After all, we'd been living like rats in a sewer. We could smell ourselves as the vehicle filled with the stench of the jungle that was seeping out of our pores. This was the first time I'd been in a vehicle other than a city bus since I was taken to jail after Tex overdosed that poor bastard in the arboretum. Hal jumped behind the wheel as Donnie explored whether he had the option of not getting in the vehicle.

"I have a hundred places to lay low, Rita. And I ain't got a big mouth. You know that," Donnie pleaded with Rita to allow him to break off from the group.

"I know you have places where you can lay low, Donnie, but for right now, you get your ass in the fucking Winnebago." Rita barked with a strong sense of command and authority. It was never more obvious that she was in complete control over her crew. She gave the orders. We were all in, and Rick had disappeared without saying a word. All of a sudden, we were headed south on I-5 like pirates on a land ship.

There was a lot of mystery involved for Maggie and me. We didn't know where we were going, what the plan was, or whether we were even part of it. Hal and Donnie certainly had more of an idea of what we were doing. Quincy and Clive didn't give a flying fuck. They were still reeling over the high they achieved from beating Tex to death. Forty-five minutes later, we turned off the freeway near the Tacoma Dome and pulled the Winnebago into an East Tacoma neighborhood. Then, into the spacious detached garage set on a large piece of property and fenced off like a bunker.

Rita addressed the group as the vehicle came to a stop in the industrial-sized garage:

"Okay, boys, we ain't gonna be here long. You can get cleaned up, and we will count out the cash in front of y'all and show you what your cut will be. You won't get the cash yet cause we need to see what type of heat comes from the show Quincy and Clive put on earlier. It was satisfying to off that little shit, but now we need to be extremely careful. So, I can't have you little sugars running around town chasing hookers just yet. We went out with a bit of a loud bang, so we need cover for now. Sure was fun, though." The group got a good laugh at the expense of Tex, and the twins glowed with validation.

"Where we headed, Rita?" Donnie was the most curious.

"We will head east over the Cascades for now. Hal knows the spot. I'm not going to tell you exactly where, but it will be comfortable. The way we killed Tex in the jungle will make the papers so we can watch from a distance for a while."

So the plan was set. We all piled out of the Winnebago into the large aluminum garage set up as a shop, motorcycle parts scattered around. It was becoming clear that Rita was associated with a biker gang. This must have been her source for the product we'd been marketing to the jungle crowd. Rick rolled up on a loud Harley shortly after we arrived. It was unclear whether he owned the property. He informed us where the showers were located and took Rita into the kitchen, where they spoke privately. Rita clung tightly to a duffle bag, presumably full of cash. Everything was happening very quickly, and the stress of these developments had my whispers singing a pretty aggressive tune.

Maggie was present with me, "Jack, are you okay?"

I was relieved to have her by my side, looking out for me. But, the abrupt changes were leading to a lot of distress. I asked Maggie if she thought it was a bad time to request Rita's assistance, my de facto psychologist. It was a stressful moment for Rita as well, and I didn't want to distract her from the work she was doing on behalf of the entire crew to serve me individually. After all, she was tasked with designing an effective escape plan. Not to mention convincing the crew that it was for our own benefit to withhold their individual cuts from our overall take.

"You will get your money, honeys. Let's not attract any attention," Rita explained her reasoning. She didn't trust us with all that cash for a good reason. Although, we had seen the cash and knew it was there.

In all of her grace, Maggie asked for Rita's help on my behalf. Rita was sitting in the kitchen with Rick having a glass of bourbon. She was thoughtful enough to break from their meeting for me.

"Okay, hon, all this has been real tough on the group. How are your voices treating you right now?" Rita probed gently.

"I'm just distracted by them. They're starting to get angry. I'm afraid they are going to start asking me to do things again."

"Okay then. Close your eyes for me, Jackie." I followed her direction, "Now take a big breath, fill your lungs all the way up, in through your mouth, and out through your nose."

We sat in a bedroom, sheltered from the world. I felt secure. Maggie was at my side, rubbing my back. Rita sat in a chair facing me straight on, up close. I could feel her breath waft into my face like a breeze from a sewer drain. Her breath may have been disgusting, but her spirit was powerful in its ability to stabilize me.

"Focus on your breath, Jackie, slow it down. Find a spot behind your eyelids, focus on it and visualize a sunset." The three of us sat in that room for forty-five minutes or so. My heart rate lowered, my anxiety waned. I needed a drink.

"You always have this approach, Jackie. It will be available for you throughout your life. It's a tool. Use it to build a stronger defense from your voices. Stand up to them. Maggie, you should always be with us while we work on this. You will be Jackie's lifeline. I want you to work real hard with him on these types of coping strategies." Rita continued to coach Maggie, molding her into stronger support for me.

I once again found myself in an incredibly supported position given the circumstances. I had a fleeting thought of my parents and wondered if I would see them again, whether I even wanted to. I remained convinced that it would be better to stay away. I would be a burden to them, a mark of shame for the family. I'd rather fade into the dark corners of society than live a life in which I was spoken to like I was special, as in special needs. I'm understood here, with the ranch crew. I'm accepted for the person I became organically, flaws and all. It was a group with a tendency to celebrate such flaws as a brand of diversity. We were a traveling support group with many varieties of dysfunction. Rita put me to work after our therapy session to distract me. Donnie and Hal had gone to Costco while I was in the session and returned with a shit load of canned goods, non-perishables, jugs of water, and top ramen. It appeared that we were headed for a remote location.

"Jackie, empty all those supplies out of the rig and load 'em up into those milk crates so we can stack 'em," Rita barked out orders to me as she removed her therapist hat and entered back into her role as leader of the ranch crew.

Many nefarious-looking characters began trickling into the garage while I was stacking the cans into the crates like a migrant farmworker stuffing bushels of cherries. Members of the biker gang. The Jokers. That's what they called themselves, and we were in their lair. I felt their presence in the room, they were predators in their own right. The Jokers circled our Winnebago like coyotes around a deer carcass. Rita appeared very familiar with all of them.

"Hands off, boys!"

Rita barked a warning as they postured toward Maggie with dirty intentions. Rita's tone of voice raised the ire of the twins, who may have ripped out the throats of these biker pricks under most circumstances. However, we were in a dangerous position, and these guys were hosting us in a sense. I'm sure the Jokers took a percentage of our jungle earnings the entire time, but we were on their turf, their property. Still, the twins were liable to take their brand of a kamikaze warrior and spray blood all over this garage.

"Ricky, get your boys out the garage while we finish loading our shit!"

It was clear we were not welcome in the Joker's garage for much longer. The conflict came to a head as Quincy postured up to one of the members and grabbed the man by his throat. The member swung at Quincy, who lifted him up by his neck and slammed him to his back on the concrete, like a WWE event. The man's head slammed against the concrete with such force that it made the sound of a hollow skull's death ring, echoing throughout the garage as guns were drawn.

"Whoa there, ya little honnies! Yall have been subsidized by our operation for the last nine months. Show some goddamn respect. Shit, we've only been here an hour-and-half." Rita took control once again with a sound argument.

At that point, Rick gave a nod, and his boys walked out of the garage, tails tucked. The guy Quincy tuned up was wobbly as hell but stumbled out somehow with a sure concussion. The twins weren't verbal shit talkers, but the look they gave those Jokers was some kind of taunt. Especially coming from the twins. These Jokers were Arian

Nation types, and the twins didn't tolerate racism at all. Anyway, I was hoping the twins would get a full shot at those bastards, only because I could see how badly they wanted it. Cooler heads prevailed, though. It was clearly not an option to remain at the Joker's garage much longer. As soon as they cleared out, we jammed into the Winnebego and were off again. It was about 4:00 pm when we headed east on I-90 over the Cascade Mountains.

Part III: On the Lamb

Chapter 12

We trudged our way up the mountain pass in that overstuffed Winnebago. Anxiety was present among the crew members. Silence accompanied us. We pulled off I-90 almost three hours into the trip near Moses Lake, Washington, onto Highway 17. It was early September, around 7:00 pm and still pretty warm in Eastern Washington. The windows came down as we got onto the rural two-lane highway. I noticed a smokey smell in the air as it had been a particularly rough summer in the region with wildfires still burning. We passed a sign indicating we were headed toward the tiny town of Warden. I'd heard of the town, having grown up 60 miles away. A sparsely populated area decorated with agriculture.

Soon enough, we pulled off Highway 17 onto a dirt road. The Winnebago rattled as we slowly headed down the bumpy, dusty path. After about 20 minutes on the dirt road, we pulled up to a triple wide mobile home with a detached aluminum garage. I noticed a camera on top of a tall wooden pole directed down at the dirt road we approached from, which was the only access point to the property. There was a large, old-school satellite in the yard.

"They said we have running water, electricity, and they even have cable coming in through that dish," Rita announced.

The vehicle came to a stop, and everyone made their way out. It was now about 8:30 pm, but light out as dusk came upon us. Appropriately, a full moon was glaring down. The Twins flopped out their dicks and pissed on the dried out turf, kicking up dust with their streams. A tumbleweed blew past. Rita approached the garage with a set of keys and unlocked several industrial fasteners. Hal assisted and slid the large garage door open like an airplane hangar. It looked very similar to the East Tacoma garage we came from. Inside were several motorcycles in various stages of repair. It was a hideout used by the Jokers. They had several hideouts like this in the Northwestern portion of the United States, with criminal tentacles reaching into various trafficking operations throughout Washington, Oregon and Northern California. Their turf ran up against the Hells Angels, who they did contract work for on occasion.

The Ranch crew had been affiliated with the Jokers throughout the Jungle operation. Other than Rita, we were unaware. They supplied the product along with an exit plan and other services to keep the operation off the radar of law enforcement. We were now taking advantage of those services. Perhaps we should have been a bit more respectful in East Tacoma. Then again, who knows? The Twins made sure we received the kind of respect we deserved, and we got what we needed and got the fuck out of their way.

At this point, we were all tired, grumpy and sober. It was getting pretty late, and the entire crew had a very stressful day. Many things occurred. We all had the chance to crash out in a real bed for once.

Chapter 13

The next morning I awoke to the sound of dishes clattering together, which was something I hadn't heard for a long time. We sat around a large kitchen table and had breakfast together as Rita disclosed some of the details about our current living situation.

"Yall put your trust in me as your leader back in the Jungle. I did what good leaders do. I had an escape plan for such a contingency as we experienced yesterday."

Quincy piped up with a rare question, "what's a contingency?"

"A backup plan, boys. What we were doing back there in the Jungle was dangerous in many ways. I have worked with the Jokers before; I get my product from them. I, excuse me, *we* had been making a 20% payment from our earnings to reserve this hideout as an option for us."

Nobody had a problem with the 20%. We were all more impressed with Rita than before and relieved.

Rita continued: "Now, we had to blow out of the East Tacoma Joker garage to avoid a shootout, and we never had a chance to count the cash before we got on the road. I'd like to do that now."

So, Rita pulled out the duffle bag and dumped its contents onto the table. It contained many bundles of cash, wrapped crudely with rubber bands.

"Just so we all understand, I'll ask you, Donnie: How much did we make on an average day?"

Donnie responded, "About $2,600, pretty much start to finish. Our customer base was very consistent back there."

"Exactly right. $2,600 per day, seven days a week, for 220 days straight! That was a pretty good run, boys." Rita's accounting seemed professional, but we already knew that. "After it all shook out, we pulled a little over 572k from the dope heads in the Jungle. 114k of that is already gone, paid in full to the Jokers who provided us with the Winnebago on very short notice and this hideout. The Winnebago is registered under the name of a member's ex-wife, who happens to look a bit like yours truly. So, I also have her ID if we get questioned on the road at some point. I have an insurance card and a registration for the rig. What I'm saying is that we got a clean rig. That's worth more than you all might think. Along with this secure hideout, as I said, which will keep us all out of jail."

Everyone nodded their heads in full agreement that Rita's deal with the Jokers for 114k was fair and necessary.

"Now, the Twins, Donnie, Hal and I will all take equal cuts."

I was curious about how this would work for me personally. Would I get a cut of this cash? I had become a contributing member of the crew by the time we left the

Jungle. But, I was more of a charity project for Rita than anything. Not to mention she saved my life and taught me to cope with my schizophrenia symptoms. She gave me a surrogate family. She even had Tex killed for Maggie and me, which immediately ended their business operation in the Jungle. From my perspective, I was not owed a dime.

"Jackie, you finished strong. You became a great member of the team. I will give you a small cut from my take in credit, and you are now a part of our crew. Does that sound fair?"

"Absolutely." I was elated that Rita had referred to me as a crew member.

"Maggie, you are, of course, part of this family, my dear." Maggie began to tear up. She hadn't really experienced this type of kinship in her entire life as she bounced around the foster care system like a pinball. It was quite an emotional moment for Maggie and me. However, the rest of the crew was distracted by the pile of money sitting on the table.

Rita went on, "Our total take was $572,000. Minus the $114,000 that already went to the Jokers leaves us with $458,000 to split. Divide that by five, equals $91,600 each." Rita split the money into equal piles of 10k bundles and unbundled a couple to cut out 5 equal portions. They all counted their individual cuts with shit-eating grins. Rita explained that they were welcome to hold the money for now, but nobody was leaving the hideout for the time being. Everyone was on board with that.

Rita had Rick and the Joker boys taking the temperature in the Jungle as well. They would let us know if the cops had any idea who we were. Supposedly Rick had a crooked cop on the Joker payroll who was able to get inside information. Everyone in the Ranch crew had a record, fingerprints and mugshots on record everywhere. If the Seattle PD had more than a couple of brain cells to rub together, they'd be able to find prints on all of us at the Ranch. That's why Rita had lined up the hideout in the first place.

Since the other guys were licking their chops while they counted the money, Maggie and I decided to check out the house and wander around the perimeter. It was pretty basic: three mobile homes stacked up against each other, forming a decent-sized rambler. It looked like a biker gang hideout. Plopped in the middle of nowhere, within a reasonable distance from Interstate 90.

"She said they have cable, right? I haven't watched TV in forever," Maggie said.

So, we went back inside, and I sunk into a shitty old couch in the living area that smelled like cigarettes and stale beer. Maggie flipped the TV on manually and left it up to fate to decide which station we would watch as she poured herself into the couch next to me. It landed on channel 4 local news. The headline running along the bottom of the screen read: "Queen of the Jungle ordered hit."

"Holy shit!" It had only been about 24 hours since Rita gave the Twins an opportunity to take out Tex, and the local news outlets were all over it. The news anchor was live from the Jungle, or what was formerly known as the Jungle. We could see cops in the background combing through the area, interviewing Jungle residents from the foot of their tents.

"Guess that 20% was worth it, eh boys," Rita shouted from a couple of rooms over with a slight chuckle but no concern. They didn't have any of our full names yet, but they had already figured out that our leader was named Rita. It was just a matter of time until they had more information, including where our campsite was, which would lead them to a great deal of identifying material. The news anchor interviewed some jumping bean who said he "knew of two guys who'd been shot to death trying to rob the crew they were looking for."

"We may need to stick around here for a couple of months and give people time to forget what our mugshots look like," Hal pointed out.

The crew huddled around the TV, clutching grocery bags full of cash. Channel 4 News was diving into the story of a matriarch ruling over a murderous crew of professional drug traffickers. The Seattle PD was probably already crawling all over the deck of the Ranch, searching through the remaining items we left: tents, food, bloody boots the Twins kicked off right before we left. Not to mention plenty of DNA they could run through federal law enforcement databases. We already knew that our entire crew had given fingerprints to law enforcement at one point or another. In fact, Donnie, Quincy and Clive were all wanted on felony charges, which was the reason they had been working for Rita in the first place. Although, the Twins would have been with her regardless. With the amount of empty beer cans we'd left scattered around the Ranch, pulling prints would be easy for the cops. All that being said, there were no regrets among the crew. Not for turning the Twins loose on that rapist. Everyone had gotten a great deal of satisfaction from that.

Rita tamped down the anxiety, "Don't get your panties in a bunch now, boys. That's why we came here, why we lined up options. Like em or not, the Jokers owe me," she hesitated, "owe us. This might be the first stop for us, but we'll get out just fine."

Donnie was curious, "Ok. Ok. You say first stop? Where will we end up?"

"Hard to say, Donnie. This crew may eventually get broken up, spread out. Our anonymity will come from our own independent abilities. So, for now, open a bottle get drunk. We have some time to kill out here, boys."

Donnie had purchased a bunch of cheap half-gallons of liquor when he made his Cosco run with Hal the day before. So, we got weird. We had all been used to drinking beer. The other crew members stowed away their bags of cash, and we celebrated. The mood was glowing. Despite the enormous law enforcement effort into locating us, we felt more secure than ever. We were used to drinking in the Jungle, surrounded by jumping beans who were crafty criminals in their own right, who knew we were holding cash and drugs. This hideout was the safest setting we'd had to get drunk for months. The wheels came off that night. We ended up outside, tossing flammable liquids from the Jokers garage into a large bonfire, howling at the moon like a pack of coyotes. It was great. We all accepted that we were headed into uncharted waters. But that wasn't an uncommon scenario for the individuals in the Ranch crew to be facing. In fact, everyone except me had faced a great deal of uncertainty throughout their entire lives. For Maggie and I, it was difficult to imagine what we would do if we were forced to split off from the rest of the Ranch crew. Rita told us earlier in the day that we were both crew members. Then she said that the group might have to split up. So, we were confused but tried to forget about that and party for the time being. We didn't know what the plan was, tried not to care.

We all woke up the following morning sprawled throughout the house after a collective blackout. My head was throbbing, frozen from the booze consumption and stuck in mental cement. We were hurting. Maggie and I shook off the hangover with a sexual encounter that was purely instinctual. Full intercourse, skin slapping like a round of applause in a special-ed class. Inside a private bedroom even. This was our first indoor sexual encounter. We felt so free, so much room to work. We were used to a small tent, so this was luxurious. The sex was the only path to pleasure we had in that moment of suffering. It was a respite from our alcohol-induced misery. It was so intense that my head was ringing even louder after finishing. Whatever hydration remained in my body had been purged.

At least Maggie and I had the option of sexual satisfaction. The other 5 members of the crew, who were used to being very active with illegal business dealings, were bored out of their minds. The Jokers had some loose weights in the garage, so the Twins would throw around some dumbbells to keep themselves from fighting each other for fun. Donnie spent a good amount of time asking the universe why he didn't bring some weed. He also killed a bit of time shooting target practice at beer cans behind the house, as we all did. Hal actually seemed pretty content just laying around under a shade tree on the property and reading whatever he could find. Hal also went ahead and got one of the motorcycles in the garage running. However, Rita didn't want him taking it too far off the hideout property out of fear of attracting attention.

Rita, on the other hand, was completely focused on the news coverage, parked in front of the television. Not out of concern for what the investigation would uncover, she knew what they would find. She conceded they would uncover our identities, even the bodies Hal buried in the overgrowth behind the Ranch. Rita was confident that no connection could be made between the Ranch crew and the Jokers. So, we weren't worried about Federal agents rolling up on the hideout in black SUVs or anything like that. Rita's confidence in the Joker's ability to protect us was comforting. She wasn't glued to the television due to paranoia about getting caught. Rather, Rita seemed to relish in the coverage. In a sense, she was finally getting some of the credit she deserved for being a female boss in an industry that's not only dominated by males, but it's also unheard of for a female to rule over such savages with an iron fist as she was able to. In a world that is not ruled by any laws but by violence and intimidation, she was able to dominate. This was how the picture was being painted by the news outlets, and accurately so.

It became a human interest piece, and Rita was quickly becoming a legend of folklore. Soon enough, the investigations being conducted by the media and law enforcement revealed the motive Rita had for ordering the hit on Tex. In fact, Tex had already developed a reputation as a predator in the Jungle circles by the time the Twins got to him. It turned out that his behavior in the Arboretum had manifested itself very quickly in the Jungle setting as well. Unfortunately, according to interviews conducted by the media with homeless Jungle residents, he'd already raped several victims in the Jungle in a short period of time. But, Rita knew that was the case when she had him killed. She could see through him from the first time she laid eyes on him. Based on what Maggie and I had reported to her about Tex, she knew that others in the Jungle would know who he was and why he needed to die. That's why she allowed the Twins to complete the task in such a public way. To send the message that rape would not be tolerated. So, when the reports began to surface about the murder of Tex being an example of street justice, that the victim, in this case, had it coming many times over, the court of public opinion ruled that Rita was not a monster. In fact, many touted her as a hero. An advocate for the vulnerable.

Of course, this was a very complicated situation since Rita herself was taking advantage of the heroin-addicted residents in the Jungle, or at least profiting from their addiction. So, all things considered, Rita was certainly being portrayed by the media in a very favorable light. And she was enjoying it. After about a week at the hideout, every member of the Ranch crew had been identified on the local news with mugshots and details about criminal history. My rap sheet was the shortest by far. As you will recall, I gave a false name after getting picked up in the Arboretum, so my real name was not revealed on the news. I was so haggard when I had been booked into jail that I knew my own parents wouldn't recognize me. The first time I saw my own mugshot, I went to the bathroom at the hideout to look in the mirror and gasped with relief. My time in the Arboretum had done a toll on me. I looked like an Auschwitz prisoner in that mugshot photo.

"Whoa wee! Jackie, you've come a long way since I wrapped your gauntly-ass in a barbeque cover so you could get some sleep after you stumbled into the Jungle for the first time."

Rita acknowledged how close to death I appeared in the mugshot as we looked at it on television. I had put on about 25 pounds since then due to a diet filled with high volumes of cheap protein and larger beer. Physically I was feeling well. But, mentally, I had to work very hard to cope with my whispers which were waxing a bit toward becoming a real problem again. The good news was that Rita had plenty of time to work with me while we were at the hideout, and Maggie was there for every second of it, receiving a great deal of training from Rita on her approach to therapy with me. This was an approach that seemed more sophisticated every day. We did a lot of meditation and worked a great deal on restructuring my internal response to the whispers.

"Just the sound of waves hitting the beach Jackie, ride them in, enjoy them, don't be afraid of them. They are a part of you."

So, at least I had something to do. But, it wasn't enough. I needed to be occupied with some kind of work. Since my participation in the sales route ended after we vacated the Jungle, there wasn't a whole lot of meaningful activity available to me. I was trying to hang in there, trying to hold it together.

Chapter 14

As Rita sat watching the local news, waiting for the next update, the anchor threw the coverage over to a press conference at City Hall. Silence screamed its way through the hideout as we all focused our attention on the television. It broadcast the Chief of Seattle Police, Carol O'Neal, standing at a podium. The headline at the bottom of the screen read: Chief O'Neal Addresses Jungle Murder.

Rita was practically drooling as she perked up off the couch, "this old rag is real ball-buster, boys. I've been waiting to hear from her," Rita couldn't contain her elation. Chief O'Neal went on to provide an update regarding the ongoing investigation of, well, us.

The news anchor was interrupted by Chief O'Neal as she began her statement... "Oh, and here we have her, Chief Carol O'Neal..."

"Good Afternoon. Ahem!" The Chief cleared her throat to let everyone know it was time to be silent. "As many of you are already aware, there has been a great deal of concern and interest from the press, general citizenry *and* members of our homeless community who are particularly concerned for their safety following the brutal beating of a homeless man in the Jungle encampment last week, which is what I am here to address. This will be brief, and I cannot take any follow-up questions. I would like to express to all concerned individuals that the aforementioned beating is now being investigated by our homicide unit, actively pursuing several leads. Our detectives have determined at this point that this was a clear case of retribution aimed directly at the victim for a pattern of abuse that individual was said to have imposed on a number of homeless individuals over an extended period of time and at a number of different encampments. We are now also investigating the vast accusations made by the individuals within this community to determine the validity of those very serious accusations. I want to be crystal clear. We are also pursuing the individuals who have been identified as persons of interest in the murder, which triggered this substantial law enforcement effort. We have not been able to determine the whereabouts of the group of individuals connected to the murder in the Jungle, but we can report that they are not considered to be an ongoing threat to the homeless population or anyone else at this time."

Rita was giggling, which was shocking to me because she had always remained a consistent, hedgy personality. Someone who was never satisfied. Even during periods when she was getting great outcomes, such as the Jungle sales operation. We extracted every possible cent out of that wasteland. But, Rita was never satisfied, always digging for more. So, I hadn't seen her excited about much of anything up to this point. Her grinding approach to life halted as she viewed Chief O'Neal's press conference. I would even say she was smitten by Chief O'Neal. Perhaps there was a bit of mutual admiration between the two of them. Both were strong female leaders, pioneers in fields traditionally dominated by testosterone and the desire to compensate for a small penis. Rita was certainly a fan of the Chief. The feeling seemed to be reciprocated in the speech given by Chief O'Neal on that day.

"I'd just love to tie one on with that broad," she announced.

Rita couldn't give it up. Her usually sound impulse control had been taken over by her desire to frolic with the police chief, who was out to arrest her. It was clear that the Ranch crew dynamics were now beginning to shift. Without Rita as our reality-based leader, we would probably fall apart in short order. I was sitting there with Maggie, seeing a new side of Rita and becoming distressed. We needed Rita to keep us in line, provide discipline and guidance. Moreover, we needed Rita focused so that she could figure out how to get us the fuck out of there.

Seeing Rita cut loose, allow herself to reach the point of sloppiness, as she did often during the first couple of weeks at the hideout, was disconcerting. I didn't feel my mental health was a concern any longer for her. It appeared that not only Rita but the rest of the Ranch crew were growing apart.

We would always have our Jungle business to look back upon. But it felt like our time as a team was over. The attitude of the crew had evolved to that of individual free agents, shopping their options, discussing what their next move may be. Our time as *'the crew'* seemed to have ended. We no longer had the sales route to bond us together. Our livelihoods were no longer interconnected.

My inclination was echoed by Donnie, who was becoming overly bored, "Rita, I know we are laying low, but the law wanted me before we started the Jungle project. I am going to need to leave before long. You know I have a number of people I could stay with while I get myself established in a new market."

Rita was no longer interested in managing personalities, "Donnie, you did well for me, but you keep your goddamn mouth shut for a few more weeks before we start talking about that shit. I can't have you popping up on the radar anywhere right now. We are on the DEA watch list, you jerkoff!" Rita was still hedging and managing risk, but her management skills were at the bottom of a whiskey bottle. Her nuanced approach to dealing with people had been removed. She was cold. Her sour approach to communication was reverberating throughout the group as the Twins seemed to be increasingly annoyed with everyone, which was scary. Without Rita reminding them to control their rage, they were liable to smash someone's skull over a misunderstanding.

"Jack," Maggie said distressedly, "Quincy and Clive are scaring me. I made them breakfast, and Clive smashed the plate in the sink because the eggs were too dry," Maggie was now seeing her lifelong pattern of becoming a victim of abuse play out once again, to no fault of her own. She had always been surrounded by dirtbags, and she continued to be. Without Rita reeling them in, the Twins were a threat to Maggie. I needed to do something. My whispers were getting aggravated as everyone else became aggravated. I fell, once again, into a deep battle with psychosis as the distress in the hideout was bleeding into my brain.

"Hal, I need you to drive into town and get more supplies. Mostly booze," Rita shouted out the front window of the rambler to Hal, who was laying under the shade tree in front of the house.

"Have Donnie or the Twins do it, Rita. I'm not moving too quick here," Hal replied.

"I can't have one of these black guys go into town around here, you fucking idiot. They'd be in the Grant County jail before they made it in the god damn liquor store. *You* look like the locals, so *you* will go to avoid problems! You got that?" Rita demanded.

Dissension in the ranks was now undeniable. However, Hal propped himself up and begrudgingly hopped in the Winnebago. Along with the changing dynamics among our crew, a different side of Rita continued to emerge. A bitter, angry person who was now pushing the other members away from her. My internal distress continued to grow.

Maggie had been in situations like this many times. She was able to place the anger coming from Rita and the frustration from everyone else into a different compartment. She was warm and supportive toward me and led me away from the group at every turn during this tumultuous time. She protected me from the group by separation. Maggie served her own interests by avoiding the group as well.

"Come on, Jack, let's go for a walk and try to clear our minds," Maggie requested.

We had been doing a great deal of hiking around the hideout in recent days, avoidance, I suppose. We took our time, imagining that we were settlers exploring the area 150 years earlier. I could tell Maggie was using the lessons she learned from Rita to help me cope with my voices. We wandered far off the hideout property one day and ran up against a vast swath of agricultural land. Beautiful circular, green crops. With a giant sprinkler rotating around them, anchored in the center as it slowly crawled around, spouting water high and far. Maggie seemed to think the crop was grown to feed the large cattle ranch in the distance. We actually sat in the dirt and watched the sprinkler circle the crop for a couple of hours. Eventually, we spotted a few farm workers making their way out to manage the crop. We decided to head back to the hideout before we attracted any attention to ourselves. At this point, we were fearful that bringing any attention to the fractured group would be dangerous because we no longer felt safe with what had become of Ranch Crew. We knew what they were capable of. We would return to this farm in the coming days as we continued to escape from the hideout and explore the countryside.

Difficult to say what Maggie was thinking exactly. I know she was laboring with full effort to support me in navigating through what was becoming an increasingly psychotic existence. I was only speaking with Maggie at this point. It was difficult to sift through the whispers and understand what anyone was saying. It wasn't the same kind of psychosis I'd experienced up to that point either. It had changed. The whispers were fairly non-directive, given how loud they were, like walking from a quiet street into a bar with a junky rock band playing a shitty song. It was a stressful point with several contributing factors. The front door to my brain opened up and let the whispers blow in like smoke from a forest fire. I was running up against it, and I had nowhere to go, no viable solutions.

One thing that was clear to me, despite my psychotic impediment, was that Maggie was fighting for me. I could see her arguing with Rita, advocating on my behalf, pointing at me on the opposite side of the room, screaming. Donnie and Hal were the most level-headed and sober at the time. Waiting, as we all were, for the heat to come down so they could move on and break loose from the group because our work together, our useful time together was over. I could feel a degree of empathy from Donnie and Hal, and I appreciated that. The problem was that the heat was not dying down at all. Media coverage continued, and Rita continued to revel in

Chapter 15

I was ostracized from the group at this point, treated as a special needs student in a high school metal shop class. It triggered my inner chimpanzee and caused me almost literally to beat my chest. I was a twenty-year-old male, of course, testosterone flooding through my veins. I became angry, and then I was a real problem for everyone. Of course, this group had no trouble physically handling me, and I found myself as a detainee, tied to a bed in the hideout. Something between a psych ward and Guantanamo Bay. I can recall the Twins handling me with relative ease, despite my best attempts at violence. They weren't as rough with me as they could have been anyway. There is a memory of Quincy lifting me up off the ground by my shirt and snatching my throat into his palm for a moment until Rita, despite her inebriation, verbally signaled to him to be gentle as he postured to slam me back to the ground. So he swung me into a rear-naked choke with the fluidity of an Olympic wrestler, allowing me to breathe and waiting for my stamina to run out. To their credit, the Twins could have beat the hell out of me, and I was asking for it. But they didn't. I was decompensated to the condition of a person in need of psychiatric emergency care once again. They would need to do something with me.

After strapping to the bed against my will, the group deliberated over my twitching body. Rita stood silent and seemed to allow the others to brainstorm, which frightened me. If she didn't have a plan, anything could happen. My eyes bugged out of my head in freight as my life was now in peril, under the control of a group of drunk, murderous criminals who were certainly capable of burying me on the property, along with whoever else had been whacked on this property by the Jokers. Tossing me into a hole and blasting me with a shotgun was certainly the path of least resistance, and I'm sure it crossed their twisted minds. Without Rita's voice in the discussion, there was no clear leader. The group hollered over each other for a few long minutes before Rita finally piped up. Despite the period of drunken dysfunction, she had just gone through, Rita snapped back into the old broad we all got to know and love. The gal we followed through the depths of the Jungle. Perhaps my condition was forcing her hand, but Rita appeared to finally consider allowing the group to separate. Her diminishing authority may have led her to decide that it was time to fire up the Winnebago again.

"Well, boys, what are we gonna do with this one?" Rita stated with her signature twine and crass. She hooked her thumbs into her belt loops and strutted around the room. It appeared that Rita was back in command. Just like that.

"You tell us. We can't leave this kid out to the wolves after bringing him along as far as we did. But we can't manage this ourselves. So, where should we drop him off?" Donnie once again showed his pragmatism.

I can recall Maggie placing her palms on the cheeks of my face. She comforted me allowed me to feel a degree of safety. The twins lifted me off the bed and moved me into the Winnebago, strapping me to a post on the passenger side of the vehicle like a prisoner of war. I was somewhat blinded at this point. Perhaps I was in some sort of shock due to the incredible distress. I couldn't hear anyone as I watched them scream at each other. The Winnebago began to move as my head banged off the post I was strapped to with zip ties. I sat crisscrossed on the floor of the Winnebego as it rumbled over the bumps on the mangled dirt road that led to the highway outside of Warden. Something crossed my scrambled mind as I sat there on the floor of the vehicle. I thought about the way I entered into this group, wandering into gates of hell and being snatched up by the devil herself (Rita) for use as a domesticated animal that could be trained.

Conversely, I thought about how I was exiting the group, and I was certain that this was my last ride as a member. That's all we were now, just a group. No longer the Ranch Crew. I was too crazy, too uncontrollable for them to continue bringing me along. They had the heart to drop me in a place that gave me a chance to survive. A place where I would be accepted and supported. Most importantly, this place was located no more than a 90-minute drive from the hideout: My parent's home in East Wenatchee.

I realized what was going on when we took the highway west instead of getting back on Interstate 5. A sense of relief came over me. I could see the familiar landscape through the windows that lined the Winnebago. The Columbia river appeared. During a session of Rita's counseling, I must have disclosed my real name and information about my parents. It wouldn't have been hard for her to figure out what their address was. Rita, of course, had a backup plan for how she would get rid of me if the circumstances called for it. A hedgy contingency plan for the crafty old gal. Not surprising that she had solicited that information for a situation such as this. She knew I would eventually decompensate to this point again, but she enjoyed the project. Her son continued to haunt her, and she continued trying to compensate for the feeling that she failed him. I was likely not the first project she had taken on to compensate for the perceived failures of her past.

We continued west on Highway 18, passing Rock Island Dam as we approached the town I'd grown up in, where I had enjoyed many advantages. Not the least of which was the incredible love and support I received from my parents. The same parents I abandoned as the illness took hold of my identity made me question everything about myself. What caused me to flee is complicated and difficult to put into words. Reality-based or not, I'd begun to feel shunned, ostracized. Of course, my altered perception pushed me toward isolation as well. The whispers compelled me to trend in that direction, perpetuating social withdrawal inside my skull. So I ran as far from the center of my life as possible into the margins. My loving parents were at the very center of my core. When I decided to flee from my life chase the whispers down the twisted path, I pushed my parents out of my mind, practically into my subconscious. The whispers caused me to do all of these things to get into the favor of an imaginary God in my mind. Even though I didn't believe in God before the whispers started communicating to me. At a certain point, they had convinced me that I would walk through a door and drop into hell if I didn't follow their direction.

I sat on the floor of the Winnebago, listening to the whispers blow like a strong cold breeze through my brain. It was at that moment that I reached a new level of insight into my illness. I began to see that my whispers tend to lead me away from my best self. They pushed me away from my strengths and planted a self-sabotaging quality into my thought process. I could see that as I watched the landscape roll by from my post in the Winnebago. It may have been fleeting, but I had some insight at that moment in time. I began to feel a closeness I hadn't experienced since the initial

165

onset of my mental illness. I could feel myself drawing closer to the home I grew up in, and I began to think about looking into my mother's eyes and feeling her embrace. The realization that I needed to feel my family's support provided me with a sense of security in that dark moment. I knew that they would help me.

I thought about my past life. The person I used to be. The thought entered my mind. It would be like to return to my life and deal with the illness in that type of setting, how my life would look. As we pulled up to the street my parents live on, the street I grew up on, Maggie approached me and squatted down to speak to me at an even eye level.

"Jack, we are at your parent's house. Rita knows where they live, and they will drop you here. I want to stay with you, Jack. I don't know how this can work, but I will walk you to the door and help you talk to them if you want."

That was the fork in the road. My mind was obviously fogged by the overwhelming sound of the whispers and the emotion from my parents' thoughts. I wanted Maggie to come with me. I wondered if it was possible for her to stay with me at their house, if she could become a part of my family, if I could finally give her the family she deserved after a life of rejection and abuse.

"Ok, Jackie, we are at your folks' house, I believe. At least, according to the Jokers, this would be it. Is that correct?" Rita was firm. My time with her was over. She swung open the side door to the Winnebago to show me the house.

"Yes. This is it," I replied.

"Well, we had a good run, my boy. I hope you get some benefit out of all the work we did together. But the time has come. Keep your mouth shut about the Jungle. I obviously know how to find you and your family." Rita's threat ensured that I would not talk about the Jungle murders. Not that I could help the cops find her or any of the Ranch Crew. They were going to be off in the wind.

"I won't, Rita. Thank you. Goodbye."

"Goodbye Jackie, good luck."

Quincy cut the zip tie that was restraining me, lifted me to my feet and led me out of the Winnebego. I stumbled out of the vehicle, disorganized, disheveled. I hadn't showered for the past several days. Maggie followed, we walked together to the front door of my parents' home. Maggie held my hand and led me to the door. I lived in this home for most of my life, yet rang the doorbell as if I was soliciting a donation for charity. I was a stranger now and didn't consider walking in unannounced. I wasn't the person who grew up in that house. I was someone else now. I didn't know if I was welcome. I didn't know what the reaction of my parents would be. I stole their car almost a year prior, fell off the

167

radar and chased my voices along a wild journey. So wild it would be hard for anyone to believe.

The crew remained parked across the street watching, perhaps making sure that I made it into the loving care of my parents. A couple of long minutes passed, a familiar squeaking noise poked my ear like a hallucination. My father walked down the hall, making his way to the front door. Suddenly, Rita had a change of plan.

"Get back!" she hollered.

Maggie and I looked back to see Rita waving us back toward the vehicle. We automatically followed her order and started running back. The twins ripped me around and wrangled me back into the Winnebego like a local rodeo competitor tying up a heifer. They tossed me into the van, and it rolled off before I hit the vehicle's floor. I never got to see my father answer the door. I was relieved. I didn't want to go back to my childhood home. An urge to flee the area reverberated throughout my body as I rolled around on the floor of the Winnebego for a few spins before being zip-tied back onto the pole. We were off. Rita clearly changed her mind. Some sort of red flag went up in that cagy brain of hers. She discovered a risk and abandoned the plan at the last second.

"Listen, Jackie, this isn't about you. I want to get you to a good place, but I can't risk having your daddy take down the plates on this bego. We're too recognizable already. Hal, take us back to Seattle. I'm going to cut you boys loose when we get there."

We drove back onto the highway, headed north along the east side of the Columbia River, made a left turn, crossed the river and continued west toward the Cascade Mountains.

"Here's the deal: we have one more job to do. We are going to get Jackie some real help with his schizophrenia. After that, you boys will get your money, and I suggest you leave Washington state."

I was confused, and the voices in my head howled like a pack of hyenas. I had trouble understanding what Rita and the guys were saying, but I understood that I was headed to Seattle and Rita wanted me admitted to a psych ward. I sat there on the floor of the Winnebego like a chained dog and pissed myself. Not because I was afraid or psychotic. I'd just been strapped to that fucking pole for so long that my dick felt like it would explode. Maggie shied away from me during the ride, which was heartbreaking. She felt the instability coming back into her life after a brief respite as a member of the Ranch crew, a pseudo-family. A familiar feeling for Maggie, it tortured her always, her response to trauma and a life of abandonment.

The twins were about to burn their money on hookers, and they were excited about that. They possess no form of impulse control, no communication skills and anxiety about speaking to women. So, they're horny as fuck. Barreling down the freeway, I'm strapped to a pole, twins writhing at the thought of a vagina, dicks are swinging in their pants. They never owned a pair of underwear. Donnie and Hal remain calmly collected as always.

Chapter 16

We approached Seattle and Rita began to bark out directions for getting me admitted to the psych ward. Donnie was going to do the talking once we got to the hospital, of course. The twins cut me loose from the pole, my wrists bloodied by the zip ties, and Quincy manhandled me to make sure I didn't start flailing around like they expected me to do. We pulled up quickly to the emergency department entrance as the Winnebago door flung open and latched hard to the siding of the vehicle. I am now standing on the sidewalk in front of a busy Emergency Room at the regional trauma center in downtown Seattle. I looked around to see several homeless men sitting at a bus stop on the corner of 9th and Jefferson. The men were speaking to the voices in their own heads. Feelings of normalcy started to set in. These men had likely been dumped out of the chaotic Emergency Room across the street after trying to seek help for something similar to what I was dealing with. This is where the local debris circles the drain of humanity. Folks come here to save their own lives, and a lot of life is tossed right back on the street from the Emergency Room.

"Ok, Jackie. I wish I could have fixed you up enough to function in the world, but you need pharmaceuticals, my dear. Now follow Donnie's instructions. He's going to get you some real help."

Rita gave up on me. Which, in her twisted mind, served to reinforce the past failures with her son and father. She would not be able to compensate for her earlier failures through her work with me. I am another example of her failure. Suddenly, Donnie was leading me to the entrance of the emergency room, reviewing the plan:

"Remember, Jack; we are here to get you into a mental ward. Cause you crazy, for real. Our story is that you were bout to jump off an overpass," Donnie prompted me.

"Ok."

I was agreeable to Donnie. I could hear voices in my head whispering vague messages; I started to feel like my voices were speaking to voices inside the brains of the men at the bus stop. I'm paranoid, feeling as though I have no control over myself or anything in the world. Donnie marches me into the chaos up to a glass window in the ER with a nurse behind it.

"I just found this guy about to jump off the Yesler overpass on I-5. He's crazy as hell. I walked him over here, so he doesn't fucking kill himself. Get him some goddamn help, lady!"

"Ok, sir. I will. Would you mind waiting here while I get things moving?" she asked.

"No. Go right ahead. I'll just wrestle this guy away from the edge again. Take your damn time!"

The nurse walked around the partition and stood in front of me, then asked, "Are you willing to come with me, sir? We'd like to talk to you, make sure you are ok."

"Ok," I replied stoically.

She brought me back to an exam room and asked me to lay down, then left the room. Another nurse came in and took my blood pressure, asked me if I'd been using any substances. I hadn't. The nurse who initially checked me in returned to the exam room and asked:

"Do you know the man who brought you here today?"

"No," I replied like a good soldier in Rita's army.

Ok, well, he left, so I guess you never will, but he might have just saved your life." Donnie was in the wind. Perhaps I never truly knew him. Meanwhile, a man approaches...

"Hello, sir, I'm here to speak with you about the reported incident earlier today in which you were seen attempting to jump off an overpass. Are you thinking of harming yourself or even killing yourself, sir?"

"Ah, yeah, I am."

"Do you have a plan for how you would do that?" The man probed.

"You just said it, jump off an overpass," I responded with indifference.

"So, you are still planning to do that?" The man continued to lead me in the direction of admitting that I was planning to kill myself with an annoying degree of indirectness.

"God fucking damn it! Yes! You fucking jerkoff. How many times do I have to tell you that? Shall I paraphrase again?" My distress tolerance was very low at this point in time.

"Sorry about the redundancy, sir. Are you currently receiving any mental health services, taking any meds?" The man was now getting some baseline information.

"Nope."

"Have you ever taken meds for a mental health issue, sir?"

"Yes, but only when I was in a mental hospital. I've never continued taking them after discharging."

"How many times have you been admitted to an inpatient mental health facility?"

"A couple of times."

"Do you know where sir?"

"No. I can't remember." Protecting my identity is something that was burned into my brain under Rita's direction.

"Ok. Well, maybe we can explore that later. How has inpatient treatment worked for you?" The man continued to annoy me.

174

"Obviously not very well. Seeing as I'm strapped to a bed listening to a choir of whispers singing behind you."

"So, you hear voices?"

"Jesus fucking Christ. Are you new or?"

"No, sir, I am not new. I have been working in this position for several years. Also, if you are willing, I am going to have you admitted to the psychiatric unit at this hospital. If you are not willing to sign off on that voluntarily, I'm going to file for you to be detained against your will due to the potential danger you currently pose to yourself. So, either way, we will be having you stay with us, in this facility, for mental health treatment."

"I'll just sign for a voluntary admit, save you the trouble."

"Appreciate that, sir. Can I bring you to the unit so they can get you started on the intake process?"

The voices in my head were screaming like a group of angry fans at an NFL playoff game. Screaming things like, "fuck off!" The general message from my internal voices at this point is to leave. In reality, I could not leave. I was now in a locked mental ward, once again. A psychiatric unit in a large urban hospital. So, it had all the bells and whistles. Plenty of psychiatrists consulting each other, residents who just finished medical school lurking around, trying to engage psychotic people into a conversation. I felt like a monkey at the zoo. But, this time, it was less offensive to my ego. I had earned some insight into my flavor of crazy.

There's a certain intrigue, an appealing aspect to the study of psychotic disorders, like schizophrenia and all of its varieties. Some people end up working in the field of mental health services because it interests them and they think it will be rewarding, fulfilling. Some go into the field to compensate for their own mental health issues. More American undergrads major in psychology than any other field of study. So, there must be something to it, right? I am not particularly interested in conversing with a resident psychiatrist who is smitten by the romance of treating someone's psychosis. Eager to prescribe magic pills and hope they affect my brain chemistry, bring me back to reality with everyone else. Fuck them. They don't know my reality. They're not inside my head, not listening to my howling voices.

However, I have no choice but to engage with the shrinks due to the circumstances. I'm honest with the shrinks now. I describe the voices. They want to help. They keep telling me. What choice do I have but to believe them? It's just hard for me to accept. Maybe it's my false sense of pride. Maybe it's the jungle mentality I adopted while running with the Ranch crew. My edgy attitude is a barrier to communication. But I'm not the only whack job on this floor with an edge. Most of them came in off the street and were on the street for big chunks of their lives. They just know how to survive at the moment, for the day. And it's not by talking about their weaknesses or deficiencies to strangers in white coats.

I used a new alias when I was admitted to the hospital so they wouldn't become aware of my County Jail records and connect me to the Ranch Crew. My third identity. A Doctor approached me with an empathetic tone.

"Jack Montgomery?"

"Yes, sir," I confirmed my new false identity for him.

"Would you mind coming with me for a moment, sir? I have some news for you regarding blood tests we have done."

I followed him into an interview room on the psych unit and sat down via his direction.

"Mr. Montgomery, your labs have come back to show that you have the contracted Hepatitis C virus."

This is not a shocker. Virtually all homeless heroin addicts get Hep C. I assume I contracted the virus while living at the homeless encampment in the Arboretum, sharing needles with the other lost souls. I was hoping that I didn't contract HIV.

"So, no HIV, right?" I asked with concern.

"You have not contracted HIV. We can actually start a Hep C treatment while you are here with us. But you will need to complete a three-month treatment, or it will actually make things worse. If you were to discharge today, do you think you could take meds every day, see a doctor for follow-up appointments every couple of weeks?"

"I don't even know where I will sleep when I leave here. Don't know where I'll eat or how I will survive. So, no. It's probably not a good time for me to start that treatment." A sobering interaction as a new reality set in.

The shrinks had me on a psychotropic medication cocktail that was starting to allow me to forget about the whispers for moments at a time. I heard faint voices in the background, but it was hardly distracting. My symptoms seemed to be giving me a break. I started to wonder if I should just call my parents and let them know I was ok. Ask for their help. As I considered reaching out to my parents for help getting back into a square life, help I desperately needed, I was approached by a woman with a guest pass pinned to her t-shirt.

"Hello, are you Jack?" She asked.

"Yes, I am."

"My name is Sarah. I am a case manager. I work for a community mental health program. Your social worker here at the hospital referred you to us for services."

"What kind of services," I asked.

"Well, we will continue working with you after you're discharged from here. We will help you to manage your mental health symptoms. But, we also want to help with other things like housing, substance use treatment. That kind of stuff."

"Do I have to?" I wondered if this was voluntary or not.

"Nope. It's totally up to you. You are not mandated to work with us in any way. I am just here to offer you services and talk to you about what we can help you with, what we are intended to do. And also what we cannot help you with." She explained.

"I'm homeless. That's my biggest problem. Can you help with that?" I asked.

"Actually, we just received a new grant to fund a number of housing placements for youth."

"I'm not a youth, though. I'm an adult."

"Of course," she responded, "but for this program, we define youth as age twenty-four and younger. You are twenty now. So, you would qualify if you decide to engage in services with us."

"Ok. I'll do it."

"Great. Let me just go over our enrollment papers, and then we'll talk more about your individual needs, such as housing. But, some of the basics first; after you discharge from the hospital, we will manage your mental health meds.

Starting out, we would like to observe you taking the meds, so we know you are taking them. Will that work for you?"

"If I have a place to stay, that will work. If I'm on the street, who knows. Probably not." I responded honestly.

"Ok, we will start working on a housing placement for you right away," she declared.

"Well, what type of placement are you talking about? What does that mean?"

"We are talking about placing you into a subsidized apartment. You would be responsible for paying 30% of your income toward rent. If your income is zero, you pay nothing. It would be your own apartment, in a building that we manage. So, full disclosure, the other tenants in the building are also receiving services from us," She warned.

It wouldn't bother me to live in the same building with a bunch of other whacks. Having my own apartment sounded great. I wasn't expecting that.

"Ok. I can take the meds and check in with you *if* I get an apartment," I confirmed.

Sarah went on to talk with me about what goals we will work on together. She inquired about my history, but I didn't disclose much. Not the town I'm from or my real name. I just told her that I started hearing voices about a year prior. And that I had been wandering around aimlessly. That I couldn't remember trying to jump off the overpass or being checked into the hospital. So, I was vague about my history in order to conceal my true identity and my involvement with the Ranch crew in the Jungle. Sarah didn't pry; she was trying to build some rapport, I suppose. Anyway, she told me she talked to my social worker on the psych unit, who said I was likely to continue inpatient treatment for two or three more weeks before they discharged me. We made plans for her to visit me again a couple of days later.

I was excited that someone was going to be available to help me after I returned to the community. I could even get my own apartment, which I had never had before, not by myself anyway. I also felt a bit of guilt, like I was leading people on. I could just pick up the phone and call my parents and have a place to go at any time. So it didn't feel right to take an apartment that someone else could be using, someone with no other options. I hadn't felt guilty for quite a while. The psych meds must be working. When my voices were really bad, guilt wasn't a feeling that came up for me. I would experience a great deal of fear, paranoia, indifference. But not so much guilt. Maybe that's because I was just trying to survive.

At any rate, Sarah had injected a bit of hope into my lost soul. All of a sudden, I had something to look forward to. I continued to work with the shrinks, recognizing that the meds I was on seemed to be working with minimal side effects. I was actually glad to be there getting treatment. Finally, I felt like I was able to fend off the whispering voices that had been fucking with me for the past year without booze or any other substance. I felt a sense of relief after speaking with Sarah. With her help, I could become comfortable in the world. I could continue living under my alias and avoid reaching out to my parents for help.

For the time being, I was stuck in the hospital in the mental health unit. So, I wandered over to the TV room to kill some time. There are a few other patients sitting around staring at the television under various degrees of sedation. I sat down at one of the circular tables, glanced around at the other patients and wondered what their mental issues were like. Do they hear voices? A middle-aged white man sitting at the table next to me made eye contact. He has a warm presence, and I can feel his desire to make a friend.

"How are you doing?" I asked curiously.

"Oh, hi. I'm well, sir. How about yourself?" The man replied warmly.

"Well, I'm doing ok. I think I'm finally on some meds that work for me," I disclosed to the man, hoping it would lead to a discussion about his mental health symptoms.

"Oh, that's good. Congratulations. Have you been struggling to find a proper medication regimen for a while?" The man asked intelligently.

"Since about a year ago, which is when they started," I responded, "I've never been on meds for more than a few weeks. I was just trying to deal with my voices without meds. But it didn't work very well."

The man chuckled, "I've been there before."

"Do you hear voices too?" I asked directly.

"I do. Yep. For about the last twenty-five years. I have some visual hallucinations too. When I'm off my meds, they start to work together and really mess with me. I've tried getting off meds too many times. Usually, after my voices convince me to stop," The man explained.

"That's kind of what happened to me. I mean, I don't see anything that's not real. But my voices didn't want me to take meds."

"Well, now that you've gotten familiar with them, you probably don't want to deal with them. I would say try giving the medication a shot for six months or so. Get used to taking them and see how that goes. I've gone off meds a bunch of times. It never works out well for me. Obviously, I've been through this mental health ward about ten times."

"What's your name?" I inquire.

"Todd, and you?" I'm Jack.

Todd and I got to know each other over the next few days. It was nice to have someone around who was comfortable to chat with. As a mental health patient, he became my mentor. Todd had been dealing with his psychosis for over two decades. He was able to provide a lot of practical advice. We just sat in the TV room, played cards, shared our observations of the patients and doctors milling around the unit. We became friends.

Before long, as Todd and I sat in the TV room bullshitting, one of the other patients on the unit changed the channel to the local news, and the headline read: "Search for the Queen of the Jungle."

"Have you heard about this?" Todd asked. After developing a bit of a friendship with Todd, I wanted to tell him that I was part of her crew. That I had been involved in The Queen's drug-running operation, and basically that I'm a badass. But I thought better of it. I didn't want to draw any attention to myself. I was thinking clearly enough at this point to know that I would need to continue guarding my identity very closely. Moreover, who would believe me? I'm some schizophrenic on a psych ward. There are probably several other whacks on the same floor claiming to be part of Rita's crew.

"Yeah, I read something in the paper. Crazy right? Have you ever heard of anything like that before?" I asked Todd sheepishly, punting the conversation back to him.

"Oh, man. Not really." Todd elaborated, "but I have a friend who became homeless and was staying in the Jungle

184

about six months back. He was telling me that there was a group running drugs through the Jungle. That they had a couple of scary enforcers, and they were a professional operation. He was impressed that they could hold down the entire Jungle as their turf. That's a rough place, with some rough characters. So, this 'Queen', he said using air quotes, must have had some big balls," Todd laughed as he said that, satisfied with his own assessment.

"Wow," I replied.

After listening to Todd talk about his friend's firsthand knowledge of the Ranch crew, I began to get a little anxious. Perhaps we were more visible during our operation in the Jungle than I had previously realized. I was now worried that someone would recognize me, place me as someone connected to "The Queen of the Jungle." We continued to watch the coverage, and I became increasingly paranoid. The news anchor continued reporting:

"Police have been able to pull some DNA from beer cans and other discarded items left around the Queen's hideout in the Jungle, which is described by other homeless folks staying in the area as 'the Penthouse' due to its large elevated deck area built from pallets and concrete blocks. However, Seattle PD have not been able to ID anyone from the Queen's crew so far. They have not found any fingerprints. It appears the group had been fairly disciplined. They had a habit of burning almost everything they were done using. Police aren't sure if that was a deliberate, savvy way of destroying identifiable evidence or just a group of drinkers who liked to burn stuff. Reporting live from the Jungle, Lyle Byrne, Ko-Ro News."

"Ha! Nice!" I responded to the report with relief.

"Man, this story has really got you excited, Jack," Todd observed.

Chapter 17

I'd been taking a proper cocktail of psych meds for over two weeks, and the shrinks seemed to have it dialed in just about right. I hardly noticed the whispers. If I concentrated, I could pick them up, but overall I was almost symptom-free. The biggest side effect I had was constipation. So, I was taking a laxative. My shit was sludge, and I wasn't able to achieve the satisfaction of a nice, big bowel movement. Other than that, no major complaints. I had started to gain a little weight but figured it was from all the sitting around, eating hospital food.

"How are you feeling today, Jack?" Asked the primary psychiatrist I'd been working with.

"Not too bad, Doc. I feel pretty stable. Looking forward to getting the fuck out of here," I responded.

"Absolutely. I spoke with your Case Manager, Sarah. So, you are planning to work with Seattle Mental Health Services after leaving, correct? They will manage your Meds, work with you on housing?"

"Yeah, that's the plan, as far as I know. I have only talked to Sarah once, though," I responded.

"Well, I just talked to her. She's coming to see you today. We are looking at discharging you in a few days. So, talk to her about where you will be able to stay in the short term, ok Jack?"

"Will do, Doc."

I had a number of things on my plate: discharging from the mental health unit, possibly getting fingered by the cops for my involvement in a drug-running operation, and I didn't know where I was going to stay when I left the hospital. This would have been enough to throw me into a full-blown crisis before I was on a proper combination of meds. But, my newfound stability was holding me in place, keeping me from spinning off into the atmosphere. I figured it was unlikely that I would be identified by the cops at this point. If they were going to find fingerprints for my second alias, Jack Nicholson, they would have.

"Hey there, Jack!" It was Sarah.

"Hey, I was hoping to see you today," I said.

"Good. Likewise. How are you doing?"

"I'm doing fine. Just a little anxious about where I'm going to stay when I get discharged from this place in a few days," I said, unable to disguise my desperation.

"Well, I have good news. We were able to secure a placement for you. It's a studio apartment downtown in a public housing building. I have the papers here for you to sign, and you can move directly in after you leave here. How does that sound?" I was shocked. I thought I would have to stay in a homeless shelter for at least a few weeks before she found a place for me.

"That sounds amazing! Thank you so much." I was elated.

"The only thing we will have to do is get you a Washington State ID for them to have on file. You don't have one do you?" She asked.

"No, I don't." This worried me. Would I be able to get an ID under my alias?

"That's ok," Sarah responded.

Now I was a bit paranoid. Is Sarah hustling me? Is she going to take me to jail so that they can lock me up? Is she some kind of bounty hunter? But I went through the papers with her, signed my fake name on the lease and agreed that I wouldn't let the streets move into my apartment once I got there, or they would kick me out.

"So, Jack, we are a harm reduction program, which means that we don't require our clients to be completely sober. A lot of the people we work with are actively using drugs and alcohol. Along with a great deal of the tenants in the building, you will be moving into. However, we would like to help people reduce their drug and alcohol use, as they are willing," Sarah explained her program's philosophy, which made sense to me. A lot of people can't just stop.

"Ok. That makes sense." Now I was really excited. I couldn't wait to tie one on in my new apartment. I wasn't feeling the urge to use any heroin. I was pretty sure those days were over. But, a nice six-pack of tall boys sounded fantastic. Sarah and I made plans for her to come and see me in a few days, to be there when I was discharged. Then, we would go to my apartment.

I had a few more days on the unit, so I continued hanging out in the TV room with Todd, passing time like two old men on a porch. I began to wonder why Maggie hadn't visited me. She knows I'm in the psych ward, right? I mean, that was Rita's plan when she dropped me off; to get admitted for psychiatric reasons. Maggie was a bit distressed during the ride over in the Winnebego, but even I got that message. And then I thought about Rita. The so-called 'Queen' would make sure Maggie did NOT visit me while I was in the hospital. No way, too much risk. Rita probably still had Maggie with her, wherever the old broad was. The Twins were certainly still with Rita as well. Hal and Donnie would have moved on to their next gig. But, the Twins would never leave Rita. And Rita definitely wouldn't let a chick like Maggie blow her cover. Hopefully, Maggie is safe, and Rita isn't too drunk to keep the Twins' horny dicks away since Maggie would be a target for those Neanderthals. These thoughts added another layer of uncertainty to my world. But the psych meds not only calmed my voices, but they were also relieving my anxiety. I just felt like rolling with the punches... whatever.

With some thoughts weighing on my mind, I decided to query Todd as to how he ended up in the psych ward with me. He'd been through places like this many times. I wanted to get his perspective, so I could avoid having to go through this again.

"Listen, Todd. We've been yapping for quite some time. I appreciate the company in a place like this. But I gotta know, how did you end up here anyway? How do you usually end up here?" I finally asked.

"Well, Jack, I get manic. And when I get manic, then I get psychotic. I mean, I have to get really manic to end up here. But I like to enjoy a little manic buzz. Sometimes I get a bit indulgent."

"You are bipolar?"

"Yes, but when I get manic, I also start to hear shit and see shit. It's crazy. Actually, it's a lot of fun. They tell me I have schizoaffective disorder. I don't know. It's a tweener. But when I idle toward mania, I feel so much euphoria I think I can do anything. It's a lot of fun. At a certain point, I just embraced it. In doing so, I end up here from time to time." Todd explained authentically.

"Do you use any meth or cocaine? Or are you just that way naturally?" I asked.

"I mean, I dabble. It's hard for me to avoid sometimes because meth and blow are so commonly used by gay men around here. So, I run into it constantly—almost every time I hook up with a dude. And I'm not gonna lie, sometimes that's what pushes me too far over to the manic side. But I've been sober a bunch of times and ended up here anyway."

"Oh, I didn't know you are gay. Sometimes I wish I was gay so I wouldn't have to deal with women," A corny joke, but I found myself in an awkward position.

"Yep," Todd replied unoffended, "I hadn't slept for several days before ending up here a couple of weeks ago. I was going hard for like a week. Just partying, going to bathhouses and fucking anyone who was interested. I guess the guy running one of the bathhouses called the cops on me. I must have been a huge pain in the ass. Bathhouses around here don't like to attract attention from the cops."

"You don't remember?" I asked.

"No, I never remember what happens when I'm that manic. I just know it's fun getting there." Todd's honesty was pretty refreshing. I continued to inquire about his history of getting admitted to mental health facilities, and he was happy to share his twisted stories. They were all pretty similar but very interesting. The next morning I was roused awake by the shrink I was working with.

"Good morning Jack. We are getting close to discharging you, my friend. Are you feeling ready to get back into the community?" The shrink inquired.

192

"Sure. I need to talk to my case manager. What's the deal with the Hep C treatment, Doc?"

"Glad you asked. I have written the order, and your Medicaid insurance will cover it. It is extremely important to take these meds every day for the next four months. The treatment costs eighty thousand dollars, and you won't get another chance at this treatment if you don't finish. Insurance will not cover it twice."

"That sounds good, Doc. I'm ready. I plan on taking all my meds and living a calm life. I'm gonna have my own apartment. I've never had an apartment by myself before. I don't want to fuck this opportunity up."

"Really glad to hear that, Jack. You do have a great opportunity to move on with your life and manage your schizophrenia well. You can live a high quality of life. Just so you know, Jack, we have given you an official diagnosis of schizophrenia. That doesn't mean that you are disabled. You should be able to manage this and live a successful life. You can work, have a family. Whatever you want. But you have to stay on top of this disorder, meaning you have to take your meds. When you get off the meds, those voices will come roaring back. You don't want that, do you, Jack?"

"Nope, I do not want that, Doc. So, can I drink alcohol on these meds, Doc?"

"Jack, you really should avoid alcohol. You are not even old enough to drink legally. But if you must, you should know that the meds will still work to treat your psychosis but will not work as well. Alcohol can flush them out of the system to a certain degree."

"Ok, good to know."

I was discharged from the mental hospital the following day. Sarah showed up right on time. I made sure I got all my meds from the pharmacy. I left the hospital thinking that I had really benefited from the treatment I received there. I felt lucky. I also thought about Rita. She drove all the way across the state to bring me to this hospital. I felt gratitude toward her once again, and I wondered what the hell she was doing. Did she have Maggie with her? When would I see Maggie again? Ever?

Sarah and I jumped onto a city bus and took it down the hill to downtown Seattle, near the courthouse.

"This is the Leopard building, Jack, welcome home."

A nice African American man greeted me in the lobby as if he was the concierge. It seemed he was a Christian type, offering to pray with people and whatnot: "Good morning, son. It appears you are new here, welcome. I look forward to getting to know you. God bless." He wasn't pushy.

I didn't have any belongings. I had on the clothes I was wearing when I was admitted to the hospital. The Leopard

194

building is an old brick high rise. I noticed it had concrete gargoyles learching on the eves above as we approached. We walked in the main entrance. There was an office on that ground floor with a bunch of staff members who were there to help the tenants in the building. It was a nice operation. As we walked up the entryway stairs, we crossed paths with a number of tenants who were distracted by their own internal voices or were on some type of drug that made them act like they were crazy. I felt a little out of place. I didn't view myself as one of these people. But I was one of "these people."

Chapter 18

Sarah advised me not to allow any company into the apartment for a few weeks. Just to give myself a chance to get a lay of the land. She told me I'd been awarded Social Security Income because of my disability. I would be given $750 a month to live off, minus 30% of which went to my rent. Plus, a $200 credit card was provided by the non-profit she worked for to "get set up."

As soon as the door closed, I began to plot my debauchery. I would troll the neighborhood for a liquor store, get some whiskey, get weird and see what happens. That 200 bucks was burning through my pocket, into my flesh. I allowed a few minutes to pass after Sarah left before going out to chase after some booze. I hadn't even sat down in the new apartment, taken in the view, and I was already leaving. Nobody knew who I was at the Leopard Building, so I was able to breeze through the lobby. I had a key card to beep myself back into the building and cash to spend.

I stepped out onto a very busy sidewalk, wearing a trucker style hat, into downtown Seattle, bordering the Pioneer Square neighborhood. I strolled down the street with a type of freedom I hadn't experienced since I started hearing voices in the Lecture Hall at the University. I had keys to an apartment, food, everything I needed. I was mentally stable and hadn't thought about my voices all day. Also, I was flying solo. I appreciated the anonymity. I didn't feel the need to be with people at all. I just wanted to be left alone with my thoughts. I stepped into the first grocery I came across, grabbed a twelve-pack of Rainier and asked the cashier to grab me a bottle of Jim Beam. He did it without even carding me.

I blasted out of the store with 175 bucks in my pockets, looking at a bunch of drug transactions occurring in front of me as I shuffled down the sidewalk, trying not to be noticed by anyone. I picked up a tiny bag of coke from some dude who was just waving it like a produce broker at a market in shanghai. I didn't have anyone watching me tonight. I could do whatever my impulses led me to.

I scurried back into my apartment and poured a glass of whiskey into a plastic cup I grabbed from the water cooler in the lobby. The first couple of drinks went down like a primer on a lawnmower, getting the fluid moving through my engine. I was going to test out my psych meds. Would they hold up to alcohol abuse? I figured I needed to blow the wheels off. I needed to find the line. How fucked up could I get without going crazy. There was so much I didn't know about my own mental illness.

The whiskey flowed, and I paced around my new apartment, looking out the window at life occurring on the street below. I wanted to feel something. The drunker I got, the more I thought about Maggie. I just wanted to feel her, to feel intimacy, be appreciated. I popped up off the shitty little couch and blasted out of the apartment, down the stairs to the 'web' room, which had a few computers for the residents to use. There were a couple of people waiting to use them, but I bullied my way through them, "Sorry, this is an emergency. I have to cut the line."

I went straight to Craigslist and started looking for hookers. I have over a hundred bucks burning my dick through my pocket, and I knew I was able to pay for pussy. There were a number of incalls very close to my location at the Leopard building. I scrolled through the options: mostly attractive African-American women, a few Asians. I couldn't find anyone who looked like Maggie, with light skin and dark brown hair. I peered out the window and saw a number of less-than-savory women patrolling the corner right in front of me. I apologized to the two guys who were waiting to use the computer I was on:

"Sorry, I was looking for a hooker. There are several right here. Have a good night, excuse me."

I don't know if it was the privilege that was hard-wired into my white-male brain or the edge I had from the jungle, but I just didn't give a fuck about the other residents in the Leopard Building. I was smug. They certainly didn't give a fuck about me either. With a false sense of confidence, I strolled out of the Leopard Building to see a bustling corner, active like an enzyme in the underbelly of Seattle. I had only done a couple of bumps of the blow I purchased earlier in the night. The whiskey was my primary indulgence. So, I had a nice party-favor to offer a typical hooker. I spilled into the active corner with a nice whiskey buzz and a brain inhibited by psychotropic medication. A combination that was new to me. It seemed that everything was always new to me.

I believe the psych meds tampered down my 20-year-old testosterone. I approached the offering of hookers. I was unrelentingly confident. Quincy and Clive popped into my consciousness. I thought about how quickly the twins would shake this entire corner down to the penny.

"Hey, hun," says the first hooker I come across.

"Hi. How are you?" I asked mechanically.

"Great, baby. Are you looking for a date," said the busty black chick with a tiny waist, short skirt, ass cheeks drooping below the view line. She had indulgent lips and perfectly-shaped eyes. I thought about Maggie for a moment, just to pay her respect. I needed relief. My dick was about to explode.

"Yes, I am. I live here. In this building. Would you like to join me inside?" I was aggressive. My Jungle instincts kicked in for the transaction.

"Oh, you are in the Leopard? Did you just get some cash from social security, hun?"

"Yep. I have a hundred left, and I would like to spend it on you."

"A C-Note will work for our first encounter, babe. I'll take a hundy off you at the beginning of every month from now on. Trust me."

Hard sell by the hooker. She was already setting up an ongoing client relationship. Seemed appropriate to me.

"Ok. Follow me." She took my hand with a soft, seductive touch to my palm. Stroking the inside of my palm with the end of her middle finger. Like the inside of my hand was the end of my dick. The sensitivity level was incredible. By the time we reached the atrium staircase in the Leopard Building, my boner was obvious to anyone who's eyeline I passed through—poking up against the crotch of my sweatpants. A sideways tent pitched with a twisted desire propping it up. I dragged her up the stairs. She walked slowly due to the 3" heels. My dick was flopping like a hungry harbor seal.

My hands trembled as I pulled the key out of my pocket and inserted it into the apartment door handle. I twitched like a crackhead as I opened the door. My date gracefully floated into the room.

"Why don't you sit down on your couch, hun?" she prompted.

I was startled by her direction and began to strip off my clothing.

"My name is Ebony, hun. We have thirty minutes. How can I get you off?" All business.

"What are my options? Suck my cock and then have sex?" I asked with genuine curiosity.

"Let me get you strapped up, hun."

Ebony proceeded to pucker her luscious lips, open up a condom wrapper and pull the rubber out, sit the condom on her lips flat and suck it against her mouth. She put the condom on my dick with her mouth, and I almost came right away. I continued to be impressed by the professionalism. Ebony cupped my penis with her mouth like a Dyson product as she slid her oral cavity down my shaft, leaving the rubber lining of the condom in her wake. As she retracted, exposing my throbbing shaft, I felt the urge to cum but closed my eyes and redirected my thoughts in an effort to get my money's worth. I didn't want to cum too quickly and look like a putz.

I could feel Ebony's tongue tickling the underside of my penis like a dragon with a fetish. Her tongue danced with skill. Even though I could barely feel her touch through the condom because I was hammered, watching her mouth, my dick pushed me to the edge of explosion. I had to pull my hips back a number of times to hold my juice.

Maggie's fallacio flashed through my mind. I imagined her gracing my cock with the delicate touch of her mouth. Then I opened my eyes and saw Ebony thrusting her face into my crotch like a jackhammer into a chunk of useless concrete.

"Slow down! I don't want to cum yet." I pleaded.

"Oh, honey. I can make you cum whenever I want. I'm gonna do you a favor and give you a taste of this pussy." Ebony proceeded to climb my torso. I was on my back, laying flat on the shitty couch in my apartment. She moved to straddle me like a python snake surrounding the breathing passage of its prey. My dick, encased in a proper condom, slid along the bumpers of her passage, stimulating my drunken cock.

I rolled her over and placed her into a proper mounting position. Missionary style, Ebony placed her hands on my shoulders, and I slid my dick into her swampy vagina. It was warm, despite the numbness from the condom. Her hands grasping my shoulders with piercing fingers, begging for a proper thrust. I stabbed away. She groaned like a professional.

"OOooh yeah. Yes. Go ahead, hun." Ebony prodded me on.

My dick was under control. Certainly, my sensitivity was diminished by the whiskey in my bloodstream. But I felt like I had control of my dick. It was going to stay hard, but it didn't need to cum. She flexed her vagina like a jellyfish in a vice and engaged my eye contact with an aggressive look, one that would pierce through a mood. Ebony flexed that vagina, tight along the shaft of my prick, and stroked me. I came within a couple of seconds. It felt like I came inside her, but the condom withheld my juice from her innards. My entire body convulsed like an alligator spinning on a meal. Ebony seemed to enjoy the eruption, which occurred about eight minutes into our encounter.

"Oooh, honey. You needed that, baby." Ebony assured me that my effort was worthwhile.

The Jiggle of Ebony's body during intercourse would remain in my thoughts and dreams for years. I rolled off of her with the hesitation of a 90-year-old Jewish man looking for his jello very delicately.

"Ok, Hun, you know where to find me next month."

Just like that, Ebody faded away, into the night. I lay contorted on my couch like I had just been in a car accident and couldn't move. I woke up in that position about seven hours later. I was pantless, hungover, and confused. As I roused myself awake, it occurred to me that I had been visited by a lady of the night the previous evening. Initially, a chuckle came over me. But, I began to feel guilty as I thought about Maggie. She was out there somewhere, probably waiting for me. I stumbled out onto the street, discombobulated, delirious.

Chapter 19

"Hey, Jack! You know Maggie has been asking around about you again."

It was Alvin, the vociferous drug salesman I had met in King County Jail after I was taken there from the Arboretum before I hooked into the Ranch Crew. Last time I'd seen Alvin was in the Jungle, right before I got back together with Maggie. It felt like it'd been three lifetimes since I'd seen that guy. He acted like we were good buds like we had just been hanging out yesterday.

"Alvin? What?"

"Yeah, man, she noticed me selling dope up by the hospital and asked about you."

"What did she say?"

"She wants you to go find her. Said she's camping up in the arboretum. She said she's at the same spot you and her shared up there before. Where all yall dope heads got hauled off to jail together. Anyways, she's in a red tent. You want some dope, Jack?" Alvin seemed to be pressing me, trying to get information.

"Nah. I quit that shit."

"So, you know anyone selling it around here?" Alvin inquired.

"Selling? I thought *you* were selling. Shouldn't *you* be looking for *buyers*?"

"I just wanna know who my competition is, Jack."

"Ah, ok. Well, no, I don't know who's selling. But just look around. Don't know why you're asking me, Alvin."

"You don't? I know the crew you were running with Jack. Just looking for some business connections, my man."

"Keep your mouth shut about the crew I was running with Alvin! I'm not fucking around, man. I'm out of the game. I'll see you around," I said with the sharp edge I developed in the Jungle.

"Maybe you will. Good luck, Jack! You seem well," Alvin yelled down the street at me as I walked away.

I briskly continued down the sidewalk, mind racing. Aggressively searching for anonymity in a crowd. Like I was running from something. I made a left a few blocks later and followed a crowd of locals toward the fairy docks. I made another right, north toward Pike Place Market, as I was struck by the joyous humanity of comfortable tourists eating brunch and drinking Bloody Marys. I considered how uncomfortable I would be if I bellied up to the bar and placed a drink order. Subsequently, I wondered how comfortable I would have been at this point in my life if I hadn't been transformed by schizophrenia.

I stood across the alley from the fish market where they throw salmon like a pigskin in a Rugby tournament. I kept a very safe distance because my reflexes were numb from my psych meds, and I was incredibly hungover. So, I didn't want to catch a pink in the chops, not that kind of pink anyway. Families laughed, oohed, and awed. I felt anonymous, so I had met my short-term goal for the day. But, I also felt more alone than ever, isolated from people in a sea of humanity. I longed for some sense of connection, realizing that Rita wasn't waiting around the corner for me to return to her bosom. I sat down on the sidewalk, the key to my apartment in my pocket, looking at homeless heroin addicts busk guitars for a dime sack. Most of them were actually very talented and enjoyed their process. They were comfortable with themselves.

It was a beautiful, clear day. My thoughts were racing. I wanted to calm down before going to look for Maggie. I didn't want her to see me in crisis again. I wanted to be normal with Maggie. I wanted to be together. I wanted to be happy enough to laugh at myself if I were to take a flying fish to the chops. I circled around the block, past all the tourist traps, and headed back toward my apartment. I needed to go look for Maggie. I was coming out of my daze and beginning to feel sober. Hoping that I wouldn't find Maggie with a needle in her arm, I scurried back to the Leopard Building, through the lobby where folks were gathered, and hiked up the stairs with a purpose. I jumped in the shower in my apartment for the first time, wanting to present my best self to Maggie. I dried off with a t-shirt and put on a new pair of pants from the clothing bank. They were way too big, but they were clean, so it worked for me. I had a belt.

I was all business, thinking that any hesitation in pursuing Maggie would tilt my fate toward a life of isolation. I was desperate for companionship. I walked down the stairs into the lobby of the Leopard Building. I looked like I was wearing a potato sack. I saw the gracious, Bible-toting African-American man:

"Hello, sir," I greeted him with a sense of appreciation as if he was a factor in motivating me on this day.

"Young man! How are you feeling now?"

"I'm feeling inspired like I want to chase love."

"Go after it, my friend! Life doesn't wait."

I knew which bus to jump on, and it took me to the U District quickly from the downtown transit tunnel. I hadn't been around the campus of UW for about a year. It had changed. The buildings were growing. It was more crowded. I stepped off the metro bus and matriculated down the sidewalk toward the arboretum. I could have traveled down the side streets and avoided humans. However, I walked the Ave on purpose. I wanted to walk past the spot where I had initially met Tex with his drug-induced slaves. As I approached the spot, I began to consider the type of evil that Tex represents and began to feel an agitation. A similar-looking crew occupied the spot. I could spot the alpha-Tex from a block away—his aggressive body language, like a silverback in, well, the jungle. A group of lost souls stewed around the Shepard like hopeless sheep.

"Hey, bud! You got any slaves I can buy!?" I screamed in his face, inviting a scrap. He reciprocated by throwing a right hook like a girl in a JV softball tournament. I felt it coming and swung to my right, pushing my ass into the side of his hip. He tilted forward just enough for me to place my center knuckle on the thin strip of bone between his eye socket and his temple, disintegrating that part of his skull. Hopefully, he ended up with a traumatic brain injury. I would never find out as I continued walking after he dropped to the concrete like a sack of shit.

I marched through the campus I had attended as a different person. I had been strutting through the halls of these buildings just a year earlier with a massive chip of privilege and entitlement on my shoulder. I attended classes paid for by an upper-middle-class family with good financials who saved for benevolent purposes. Now I was strutting down the Ave as a person who has nothing to lose, who is pushing down the sidewalk through shadows left by my psychosis, reflections of my whispers disguised behind the veil of psychotropic medication. I was relieved to know that my violent streak, the Irish bones in my body, were not significantly diminished by the meds.

My perception was reminiscent of a movie lens as I continued past the rest of the bars on the Ave. It was influenced by the adrenalin pumping in my veins. I was exhilarated. But, I was also masked a bit by lack of sleep and feelings of desperation. People leaned away to allow me a wide berth as I moved toward the south end of the Ave, where I had stayed in a homeless shelter after being cast away by my roommates after stealing my parents' car on a clean break from reality.

I was clearly presenting as a man without a family or anything to lose based on the response from the yokels as I stomped past them in search of Maggie. Marching toward the margins of a very large university campus, into the Arboretum where I intended to find my long-lost love. I passed through the Japanese Garden, where one would find solitude, and began scanning the undercarriage of the park. The tree beds, hollows. Anywhere an encampment could take place as I was unable to recall the exact location of Tex's sanctioned campsite. It was close enough to jump up and bite me as I veered off the trail, smelling a waft of soggy humanity. I wandered over an embankment, to a hidden tier of land, halfway down a ravine. This was not the arboretum encampment I had laid down in. Instead, I hiked into a similar village of tents, much better camping real estate. A John-Wayne-looking-elder stepped in front of my path as I moved closer.

"Hello, sir, what's your business here?" He asked respectfully.

"Looking for my partner, Maggie."

"Maggie? Not sure you've got the right camp. But, I may know who you are looking for," he said as he looked up to the sky, pondering while he tugged on his beard.

"She's in her early twenties, brunette, could be pretty tore-up if she's back to injecting, which she probably is if she's camping around here," I described Maggie.

"That's a dime-a-dozen, son. But, nobody here hits that name with that description, to my knowledge. Let me check with the primary dope dealer and get right back to ya."

I waited at the entrance of their encampment like I was in a shoe store, waiting for the employee to see if they had my size in the back.

"I consulted the most prominent dealer on our bluff. He thinks the person you are looking for is a few hundred yards south of here, staying in an orange tent. One that used to be red until rain beat the tart out of it. So, you are looking for a cheap trick, eh?" The old man asked in an enterprising way as if he had another cheaper trick to refer me to.

"No! I don't know. Maybe I am. Sometimes. I don't know how desperate she is. That's why I need to find her. I care about her."

"Oh, ok. I didn't know you cared about her. Just thought you were trying to get your noodle wet like most of these jerkoff-johns that wander in here. Let me help you. I'll bring out my dealer. He's got the silver tongue. He can help you find a worm in the ground."

I was agreeable as I watched a familiar-looking black man emerge from the layers of tents that this encampment had annexed from the Arboretum proper.

"Donnie?"

"Oh shit! Jack! Mothafucka. You made it out of all that."

"Oh my God! Donnie! It is you. Ya sombich!"

We embraced like long-lost brothers. He entertained my connection to him as if he cared about me on some level. It was no surprise to find Donnie in a similar job as the efficient dealer to a large number of junkies at an under-the-radar encampment.

"So Jack, you are looking for your girl Maggie I assume?"

"Yessir."

"I gotta be honest with you, Jack. She's been doing what she's got to be doing to survive, my man."

"Donnie, I hear you. I figured as much. Can you help me find her anyway?"

"Look here, Jack, I'll bring you straight to her. Let me just grab my pistol before I leave this encampment."

Donnie was not comfortable exposing himself to the general public without carrying. As per usual. I felt a level of security being around him. I could let my confrontational side rest. Donnie was around, in control. Just follow his lead. The aggressive posture I enjoyed on my walk down the Ave reverted back to a follower as Donnie led me to the main Arboretum path. He tapped me on the small of my back as he marched past me, like I was his bitch, as he made his way back up the hill toward the main path in the Arboretum, the primary thoroughfare. We emerged from the thick brush and stepped back onto the path with the wandering 'normals' who were just out getting fresh air. I typically tried to blend in with the privileged white Seattlites. Donnie definitely didn't give a fuck. He just wanted to get off the main path quickly and back to the underbelly.

The paved Arboretum pathway acts as a line of demarcation. On the dark side of this path, the encampments would be less civilized. We ducked back into the brush on that side of the trail. Donnie zipped up his best attire like a Nike commercial, and we pressed on with his swagger cutting through the bush. Donnie didn't need anyone to back him up. Donnie would explode on a buyer like they broke a federal law if they didn't have clean cash in hand. Donnie was a disciplined shark. Plus, he had a number of firearms concealed beneath the baggy, baby blue sweatsuit he was wearing, which was a different look than he had presented to the Jungle crowd. He didn't want to be recognized. A fucking chameleon. I followed Donnie's swagger. He didn't care if the junkies recognized him. He wanted them to. He was trying to avoid recognition from the square world, from the law.

"So Jack, you on Psych meds now or what?"

"Yep. Took them this morning. Every morning for over a month, every damn day."

"That's good, man. You were getting better, but when their voices start popping off in yo head, you gone."

"I know. I'm gonna stay on the meds. I got an apartment from a mental health program, so I feel kind of obligated."

"No shit? Good for you. They probably felt obligated because of your whiteness. You know how many crazy brothers die on the street?"

"Yeah. You're probably right about that, Donnie."

I slumped behind Donnie, weighed down by a bit of white guilt as he kept me on my heels, establishing himself as the clear alpha. We continued moving through the brush on a trail so hidden the Vietcong would be impressed.

214

"Hey Donnie, I'd want to do whatever I could to make up for my whiteness."

"Oh, you do, huh? Why don't you go off and pick some fuckin cotton while you get whipped then?"

"Sorry, I just wanted to…sorry."

"Just trot yo fragile white ass behind me and don't get fuckin lost, Jack."

It was clear that my status as a Ranch hand had not changed. Donnie was doing me a favor to bring me to Maggie. My thoughts were absorbed by Ranch crew memories as I followed Donnie with my palms up to protect myself from the thick shrubbery. We swam through branches and leaves and broke through into a canyon of trees with large Evergreens separating like a river valley. Donnie struts out of the bush and into the canyon encampment like Richard Prior. I peered over his shoulder to see a camp so hidden it was like a homeless oasis.

Chapter 20

The Canyon Encampment is clearly a youth village. Late teens to early twenties. I suddenly felt comfortable as we worked our way through a neat row of tents elevated above the dirt by double-layered pallets, zip-tied together for foundational support. These kids were obviously receiving support from the bleeding hearts at the University who can't help but approach the homeless youth population with resources. There were several volunteers working to clean this place up. This was an encampment model I was not familiar with. Dripping with undergrads volunteering their time. I felt the protection of the government as I followed Donnie down a network of paths, crisscrossing a large, youth-occupied encampment in the tree canyon.

Donnie strolled past meticulously crafted campsites with coffee tables set along the path. Donnie was familiar with this camp. He sold products here. If I had ended up in this encampment instead of getting dragged into Tex's camp, perhaps my path would have taken a different direction. I had never gotten hooked into the youth services. I stayed at the youth shelter for a couple of weeks but didn't engage with them. Rita plucked me up when I was vulnerable and groomed me into a Ranch-hand to work on her heroin distribution team under Donnie. Hat in hand, I was asking my former supervisor for a favor in helping me locate Maggie.

We approached a three-foot path around a tent lined with gravel, sitting on a single pallet. Donnie stopped walking, turned back toward me, and directed me to the tent-like Bob Barker introducing a new car:

"This is it," Donnie said with a pointed hand.

"Maggie?" I called out like a desperate boyfriend.

I received no verbal response. However, there was a great deal of frantic rustling in the tent reacting to my call. Two people were inside the tent based on the amount of movement. I looked back to Donnie as he showed me his palms in empathy.

"Hello?" I was confused.

A man emerged from the tent and scurried off, avoiding eye contact.

"Jack?" Maggie poked her head out of the tent, and we locked eyes. "Jack! It is you!" Suddenly we were wrapped in each other's arms.

"Maggie, who was that guy? Are you with someone else now?"

"No, Jack. I need money. That's what I was doing. That's how desperate I've been!"

I was initially stunned to think that Maggie would fuck customers for cash. Then I felt guilty for thinking that. I'd been fucking a hooker myself a few hours earlier.

"Do you still love me?" I asked.

"Yes, Jack! I'm just trying to survive here."

"Well, I fucked a hooker last night, so I guess I can't judge."

"What!?"

"Yeah, I feel guilty about it. But not that guilty now that I know you are a hooker!"

"What? Fuck you, Jack!"

"What do you mean fuck me? Fuck you, hooker!"

Donnie chimed in: "Good to see you, Maggie. Good luck, love birds," Donnie turned and started to make his way back to where he came from. I knew where to find him. He disappeared into the brush. Maggie and I were left to deal with our awkward situation without a mediator.

"Maggie, I still love you," I pleaded.

"I don't want to fuck these guys. I just want to live," Maggie scrambled to preserve her integrity.

"Yes, but you just fucked a random junkie."

"I did. I am a hooker. An easy-to-get hooker. I needed to get money! To live. You idiot."

Obviously, Maggie was on the right here. She was a person just trying to survive, making money the only way she knew how. The oldest profession in humanity. But, she *was* ultimately a hooker.

"Maggie??! What do I have to do to get you on board with me?"

"On board? I don't know! What the fuck are you talking about?"

Maggie and I continued to argue belligerently for several minutes. I eventually remembered that she was a broken person, as was I. She was merely meeting her own basic needs through prostitution. I tried to extend to her the grace she had provided to me. After all, she stuck with me through difficult times.

"Maggie, I have an apartment now. Fuck this tent. Come live with me. Sleep in my bed, honey. You can stop doing all this."

"What?! Jack, I only want to be with you."

Maggie is a damaged person. Man-made damage. Not like me. I'm psychotic organically. It has nothing to do with my life experience. It would have happened regardless of my situation in life. Otherwise, I was just as privileged as the next frat boy on the row. I hadn't experienced trauma like Maggie. She's been raped and abused throughout her entire life. Her prostitution was a continuation of this traumatic chaos. She began to gather her belongings. I helped her carry some bags of stuff. We toted a load of garbage bags back toward the arboretum trail.

"Maggie, is this stuff worth schlepping all the way downtown?"

"Is your apartment downtown?"

"Yes."

"Oh damn. Ahh, this is mostly junk. I don't care about this shit."

So we left all of Maggie's belongings behind. She joined me with only the clothes she was wearing. Hand in hand, we strutted back toward the Ave. My mood had swung over the past couple of hours since I'd pranced down the Ave like Bruce Lee. I was more subdued. In fact, I was in a nesting mood. My objective was to get Maggie back to my apartment and set up a stable life together. So, I took the side streets on the way back to the bus stop to avoid seeing the second-rate Tex I had leveled with my best punch a couple of hours ago. I didn't want any more trouble. I had in my possession what I had come to get: Maggie.

"Jack?" I heard a familiar voice calling out from blocks away. But they couldn't be calling for me. Nobody around here is looking for me.

"Jack!" I turned to see my old roommate Bryan jogging in my direction.

"It is you. What are you doing? Dude, we all thought you were dead. So do your parents."

When Bryan started speaking to me directly, I was taken aback. I didn't want to see him. I just wanted to get Maggie back to my apartment and begin living our lives under the radar, away from people like Bryan. I wasn't the person who Bryan thought I was. I had changed. I was someone different now. So I pretended that I didn't know him. I pretended that Bryan was mistaken.

"You got the wrong guy, bro. I'm not Jack. I don't know you!" I hollered this message so firmly that Bryan took a step back as if he felt threatened.

"Oh, sorry. I'm sorry." He started an apology out of reflex. Bryan was perplexed. Also, I had scared him with my tone and body posture. And then Maggie ruined it...

"Jack, he knows your name. He obviously knows who you are. What are you doing?" Maggie was understandably concerned about why I was disguising my identity from Bryan. I was now wedged between a rock and a hard place, trying to figure out how to hoist myself out. Bryan was still standing there, staring at me with his jaw hanging down to the sidewalk like a cartoon dog.

"Look, man! I used to be someone you knew, someone you were friends with. I'm not now. I don't know you. So fuck off!"

With that, I grabbed Maggie's arm and yanked her down the street, leaving both Bryan and Maggie miffed. Neither of them understood why I was concealing my identity. And they were confused for very different reasons, seeing the world through their own lenses, on opposite ends of a spectrum. Maggie had no shame and didn't care. So, she would never be anything but authentic. She didn't have the ability to lie to her own detriment. Bryan, on the other hand, couldn't understand why I wouldn't want to be normal again. The truth is, I didn't understand it either.

So, I marched on with Maggie in my grasp. We walked past Bryan, who's mouth remained open, and stomped toward the bus stop like soldiers trying to make it back to their homeland. We boarded the bus looking disheveled. My mental health case manager had given me a free bus pass. But Maggie didn't have any bus fare. So I pleaded desperately with the bus driver to let her ride for free. But he wasn't hearing it, "Son, I'm not that kind of driver, sorry. Get on off now," the pale, splotchy old bastard flaunted his tiny bit of authority in my face like a dictator. We got off and waited for the next bus, who's driver was more sympathetic and let Maggie on for free.

The bumpy ride kept Maggie from nodding off as we made our way downtown. Her eyes were rolling back in her head from heroin use. I gripped the hood of her sweatshirt and twisted it like a rope to make sure she didn't tumble forward onto the floor of the bus like a flaccid penis.

We exited the bus in the downtown transit tunnel and made our way up to the street. My apartment was only a few blocks away. I dragged Maggie along the sidewalk by her armpit like I was dancing with a manikin. She was coherent, however, sedated. As we crossed 3rd Avenue toward the Leopard Building, I could see the de facto doorman working the room, eliciting smiles from everyone in his bubble. I would need to pass through that bubble to get up to my apartment.

"Maggie put on a happy face for a few minutes. This guy wants me to find love but won't let me bring a doped-up hooker into the building. So, clear up for a few, eh?"

"Ok," Maggie said as her posture propped her chin up, and her supple breasts perked like meerkats on the sahari. "Oh, my Jack. Can I live here with you?"

"Of course! That's why I dragged you down here. Now we can start our new life together."

"No shit?" Maggie was still not convinced that I could provide her with a leisurely lifestyle. Her doubts were understandable, again, given my disability status as a mentally ill ward of the state.

"Jack, nobody has ever tried to take care of me before. So, it's kind of hard for me to believe you. Do you just want to take care of me? That's what a pimp says." Maggie's history of trauma made it hard for her to believe that I just wanted to be with her. And make life easy for her. She'd heard that before and couldn't buy that line of bullshit, however authentic my intentions were.

"Maggie, I *am* serious. I just want to be together. You can live here with me, and that's it. I don't want anything else for you. I'm not going to try to get you to turn tricks for me or anything else. It's really just simple: I love you and want to be with you."

"Oh, ok, Jackie… Can I get a nice tea to put me down then? What are you, a pimp or a butler?" Maggie asked with a thick tone of resentment. It was becoming unclear as to whether Maggie was capable of living a peaceful life of cohabitation. To her credit, she was withdrawing from heroin. So she deserved a little patience. I couldn't help but wonder, for the first time, whether Maggie was capable of being happy. Or if she was so used to being abused that she expected to be treated poorly. Perhaps my attempt to help her realize a higher quality of life could never be accepted? Maybe she was unable to believe she deserved a peaceful, happy life.

We breezed past the doorman, who graciously pretended not to see me bringing in someone from the street. I finally got her up to my apartment and had no choice but to give her a little time to get used to the idea of living with me in our own dwelling. To give her time to get over the dope-sickness. We sat on the frayed couch donated by the goodwill, staring at the wall. Trying to feel comfortable in our own skin. A knock on my door interrupted the cold silence and echoed through my squeaky 1920s apartment.

"Who the fuck is that, Jack?" Maggie inquired as politely as she was capable of at the time.

"I don't know." I got up off the couch and approached the door slowly. "Who is it?" I asked in my best version of a baritone.

"Hey, Jack. It's me, Sarah." It was my mental health caseworker. She probably just wanted to make sure I was taking the psych meds. "Can I come in?" Sarah asked directly.

"It's not a good time. I have a guest," I responded with avoidance.

"Oh, ok. Can you bring your meds over to the door with a glass of water, crack the door and let me see you take them? Please. I just wanna make sure you continue taking them as we have talked about so that we can continue making progress."

She was a persistent little shit. So I complied. I was fortunate, of course. With everything else that had occurred, I hadn't even considered taking my evening meds. Sarah could have easily just backed off when I told her I had a guest. But I needed a firm hand to guide me. I'll always appreciate her effort and skill.

"Who the fuck is that, Jack? Another Hooker?" Maggie chimed in.

Maggie approached, and soon the three of us were standing in the doorway, staring at each other. Sarah handled Maggie's agitation well.

"Hi there. I work with Jack. I'm his caseworker. I'm not trying to give you a hard time or anything," Sarah said, providing Maggie with some context as I swigged the pills down, "Well, have a good night, yall. I'll check up on ya again tomorrow, Jack."

With that, Sarah swung the door closed, and she was off quickly. But not quite quick enough because Maggie had a chance to find something to be offended about.

"Oh, is that your little medication manager Jack?"

"God damn it, Maggie, I know you feel like shit, and you don't believe that I want to make you happy, but don't drag me into misery with you. I want to be normal!" I shouted in Maggie's face.

"Normal? You think I could ever be normal? You think you could be normal? You're a fucking schitzo, Jack. A nut job! And I'm a damaged whore with so much PTSD I have to sleep with my hand on a knife. Misery loves company, Jack. Our company isn't normal."

Maggie had a point. Maybe I was delusional in thinking that the two of us could live happily ever after. My own instincts, which were inhibited by psychosis and sedative medications, were triggering a warning in my head. Like an evacuation, an alarm was echoing through my head, telling me to get the fuck away from Maggie and move on. At the same time, I believed I was in love with Maggie. Just yesterday, I longed for her, aching to see her and feel her.

So I asked, "What do you want to do, Maggie?"

"I don't know, Jack. You think you can just move me in here and start some kind of American dream life. But we don't have the privilege of dreaming. We are just trying to survive. You can't even remember to take your crazy pills without someone coming to your door to remind you." Maggie made clear how hopeless she was.

The wheels had come off pretty quickly for Maggie and I. Maybe we *were* only good at surviving together. Now that I was off the street and able to think clearly because my voices were hushed by the meds, I could see that our love for each other was situational. A union of convenience with utility meant for the deep underbelly of society.

"Jack, can I get five bucks? I can't stand it. My skin is crawling."

Maggie further reinforced my suspicion that she was a slave to the needle. First, everything else in her life followed

227

heroin on her hierarchy of needs. She wasn't going to be able to stop, even if she moved off the street into my apartment.

"No, I don't have any money. I spent my entire social security check on booze, crack, and a hooker last night."

"All of it? I just need a small hit," she begged.

"Nothing."

"Ok, well, I'm gonna hustle for a fix then."

"Good luck," I wished her well.

"Should I come back, Jack?"

"Don't come back, Maggie. We're headed in different directions. Let's just both move on."

The end of our relationship was upon us. With that, she was gone, scurrying out of my apartment like a rat heading back to the sewer. I wasn't even upset, just relieved. I knew I wasn't strong enough to drag that kind of baggage along with me in life. I needed people to push *me* along, for that matter. I have all kinds of support needs. The good news was that I could focus on myself and try to recover now that I wasn't hung up on Maggie. Whatever that means.... to recover. Confusion filled my brain as I found myself alone once again on an island, isolated.

Chapter 21

-Knock-Knock-Knock-

The knock on my door was clean like a high school marching band had just entered the room. It echoed throughout my hollow caverness apartment. I assumed it was Maggie crawling back like a shameless roach.

"Who is it?" I asked with annoyance toward Maggie, but it wasn't her.

"It's Sarah. I was out here in the hall that whole time. You okay?" she asked empathetically.

I was not surprised that Sarah had seen this coming, waiting quietly in the hallway for one of us to storm out of the apartment or worse.

"You heard all that then?" I asked through the closed door.

"Some, or maybe most. I delivered meds to a different client upstairs in the middle of your arguing. But yeah, I got the gist of things."

I cracked the door and peeked out to see Sarah crack a smile. "Come on in." I requested.

"How you doin buddy?" Sarah asked in a folksy, endearing way. "that sounded pretty emotional..." Sarah jumped right into the world I lived in with Maggie.

"Ah, yes. It's good, really. At least we didn't string each other along through a bunch of bad times before we realized it wouldn't work. I just fear loneliness." I opened up.

"You are pretty isolated, Jack. What about any family? You've evaded questions about family or any human connection at all. Do you know how to reach your family? Your parents? Are they alive? Do you even know? We can call them together. I'll help you." Of course, Sarah was right. I should call my parents. But the invisible force preventing me from doing that, the shame and stigma I felt, was strong. I didn't want to be vulnerable to them in that way.

"Let me think about that," I told Sarah in response to her offer to assist me in reaching out to my parents.

"Fair enough, think about it. I'm available. I'll touch base with you tomorrow. I hope your night takes a stable turn, Jack." Sarah was off into the night, on her way to make contact with other mental health patients on her caseload.

I found myself alone again, isolated. The whispers in my head made their presence felt due to the distress I was feeling following my breakup with Maggie. My psych meds were strong in their battle to hush the whispers, but the muffled sound of distant voices was present for me that night like adolescent brats whispering into a bull-horn from the alley below my apartment, amplified as if the sound was traveling underwater. Like I had dipped my head into the ocean and heard a whale giving birth nearby. The whispers tortured me that evening with malice intent. I struggled to cope, thinking back to my lessons with Rita in an effort to deal with them more effectively. But, they continued on, like petulant children teasing me, urging me to jump out of my apartment window, "just let go, just fall to an end."

I had enough insight to recognize that I'd been through a lot over the previous hours, and I didn't want to die. I had no intention of submitting to the suicidal commands in my head. I paced around the apartment, considering my options. Heroin was toward the top of the list. It would allow me to escape very easily and quickly, the voices may continue if I were on heroin, but my consciousness would float out of my body and not be affected. But that was too easy, I was committed to living, and heroin was equivalent to suicide. I didn't desire that opiate destruction.

I considered booze as well, which was very appealing. But I had no money, and I was coming off a wicked bender. So, I realized that wasn't the best decision either. Then I thought about calling Sarah for support when I began to hear a female voice in the hall cursing at something.

"God damn. I can't get a thing right!!" the voice stated as it trailed off into a high tone of hopelessness I could relate to. I swung the door open with little self-awareness and shot my glare toward the woman who was struggling to navigate her apartment key into the deadbolt lock.

"How ya doing, honey? I don't know shit about this place just moved in today. I can't even get my fuckin door open, and I have the key in my hand," she was endearing. Her self-deprecation was very disarming, and I liked the cut of her jib.

"I'm not doing very well either," I assured her, "but I can probably get your door open if you want." She handed me the key, and I slid it into the keyhole like a knife through warm butter and opened the door for her.

"There ya go. Make that look easy, sweetheart. Why don't you come on in and be my first guest. I'm not much for being alone. I'll take any company. So don't be too flattered," she said with a ball-busting smirk. I could tell she was no dummy, just not domesticated enough to know how to unlock a door.

"Okay," I said with a degree of relief, "I just moved in here too. It's been okay. I'm just crazy, so maybe it's hard for me anywhere." She plopped down onto a squeaky wooden chair at her kitchen table. The only other piece of furniture remaining in the apartment was a mismatched Adirondack yard chair on the other side of the table.

"What kind of crazy, sweetheart?"

232

"I hear voices, schizophrenia," I sat down in the yard chair and slid comfortably back.

"Oh yeah. Got a lot of good friends from the street who hear shit inside their heads too. Some are worse than others. You take meds for that?"

"Yeah, I take em. They work pretty well mostly. How long did you live on the street?"

"Oh shit, most of my life. I had a family growing up but left around 12 years old cause my Daddy couldn't stop beatin on us. Especially my momma. He eventually killed her, and we were out on the street, three of us. I had two younger sisters. They went into homes, but I was old enough, maybe ornery enough, to take to the street and try to make it on my own. How bout you? How'd you end up in a place like this? You look like you came from good stock, probably have family, right?"

"I do, but I haven't talked to them for over a year. They don't know who I am. Actually, I changed my name. Or I gave a fake name when I went into jail about a year ago, so they would have no way of finding me."

"Hehe, the old jail switcharoo," she said, chuckling, "I did that once myself. Long time ago, the first time I went into jail, actually. Kind of easy, really, ain't got no ID, they ain't got no prints cause you ain't been fingered yet, so you ain't got nothing to lose, why not, right? But it only works

233

once cause now they got your prints from when they booked you in."

"Exactly. That's what happened. I just figured why not. And then I just left my old self behind. Well, it was already gone anyway once the voices started."

"Well, shit, honey. Now yur settin here with me, a recovered bum," the woman said honestly. She was in her mid-forties. A little worse for the ware, she had slumped posture, her eyes drooped. She was skinny, wearing a tank top, no bra. She had heavy bandaging on her right shoulder.

"What happened to your shoulder?"

"Oh, just an old abscess that keeps popping up. I don't shoot anymore unless I really need pain relief. But you saw me try to unlock the front door. I can't hit a vein with a needle, so I just muscle right into my shoulder. I'm a boozer mostly. What's your poison?" She asked to change the subject.

"Booze too. I've dabbled with heroin, but whiskey is my main thing. What's your name anyway?"

"Oh, I'm sorry, honey, I'm Desiree. Look, I got some cheap whiskey if you wanna catch a buzz with me." She pulled a half-gallon of Black Velvet from her backpack.

"I'd appreciate that, Desiree," she didn't ask my name as she poured whiskey into a couple of plastic cubs that were already on the table we had been sitting around. Desiree is

234

Caucasian looking. She had the remnants of teeth in her mouth, just barely like dark nubs flush with her gum line. Her lower lip hangs low, showcasing her infected mouth. I chose not to inquire about the teeth.

"I don't know about this place," Desiree announced. "I might be more comfortable under a park bench."

"Why is that Desiree?" I made a point to state her name since she had yet to know mine.

"Too much PTS," she said.

"What's that, Desiree?"

"Post-Traumatic Stress. I been beat up and raped so much that I can't sleep in a place like this. All this noise coming in from the hall. I'm used to camping deep in the woods, where I can only hear the birds and the rats."

"Damn. That makes sense. So, this is your first night here?"

"Yep. I'll give it a try. My caseworker wants me to stay here to get away from my husband because he beats me up so much," her eyes started to tear up, "I love him so much, and he just beats on me. I know he loves me too. But when he gets to drinkin, he gets mean."

"Is he coming here tonight?" I asked with self-preservation in mind.

"No, he doesn't know that I came here. I never told him. I miss him, but he would kill me, just like my momma. We are cursed, I think."

"What kind of curse?" I asked with genuine curiosity.

"We only love men who beat us." She shook her head so quickly that her lower lip swung like a flag in the wind and brought herself out of the sadness like she was changing into a different person or personality.

"Anyway, what did you say your name was?" She asked finally.

"I didn't yet. My name is Jack."

"Is that your real name then?"

"That is my real first name, yes. My caseworker convinced me to come here too."

"No shit? Well, I'll tell ya, Jack, it's nice to have an option of being housed. Nobody offered me an apartment for twenty years until I came across my caseworker. She worked pretty hard to convince me to move into this place. She was always trying to get me to file police reports against my husband and all that. I'd never do that, but we do agree that he will eventually kill me. He's in jail anyway, so I thought it was a good time to try this housing thing out."

"What's he in jail for?"

"Oh, he beat some guy up. Assault. Probably. I don't know," she said, rolling her eyes.

We continued drinking and shooting the shit. It was a welcome distraction for a couple of lost souls. I eventually stumbled back over to my apartment and passed out. I made it through the night without throwing myself out the window, so that was a success, just to survive.

Chapter 22

I awoke the next morning in a contemplative state. I was weighing the pros and cons of my current situation. Should I remain at the Leopard building in lieu of the growing sense of community I was feeling with Desiree next door? Or should I just throw in the independence towel and call my parents? I walked into my kitchen and turned on the faucet to fill a glass with water. The faucet burped as the water crawled from below the street, up the pipes of this dilapidated building, collecting lead, no doubt. I peered out the kitchen window onto the busy street below, thinking about how close I came to plunging to my own death on that street the night before.

It was a new day. I fingered my mediset and popped open the next days' worth of pills. I wasn't sure what the actual day of the week was, but it didn't matter. I swallowed my daily psych meds and sat down on the couch, starving. I staggered down the stairs into the lobby of the Leopard building and approached the front desk staff, who were fresh out of a bachelor of a social work program, hearts bleeding, but no real skills.

"Where can I get some free food? I'm broke and hungry," I stated very directly to the gal behind the front desk in the lobby.

"We serve breakfast in this building, sir, right over there through those doors." With all the chaos of the previous few days, I'd failed to realize they offered free food at the Leopard building.

I meandered toward the food as directed. The room was filled with drug-addicted mental patients who were generally combative. A man stood in the food line berating staff about the quality of the food, "I wouldn't feed this to a horse!" He shouted as he accepted servings from the kitchen staff. I entered the line and grabbed a tray. They were serving scrambled eggs and toast. Some fruit was available as well. It wasn't terrible. I soaked the eggs in ketchup and hot sauce, which was also provided. I couldn't bring my tray up to my room, so I ate at one of the cafeteria tables and moved on.

With food in my belly, I stepped out of the Leopard Building onto the street in the light of day. There were crowds of people moving down the street, dressed in business attire. The square community was headed to work. I was jealous. I felt disconnected from that side of life—the side where people are motivated to work and accomplish things in the world. I wanted to be a working professional but realized I was nowhere near such a reality. I matriculated down the street and into the herd of humans moving toward their obligations. I looked around in envy at the professionals who were headed off to Amazon headquarters, or to an accounting firm, or a law firm. I decided to walk into the bus tunnel and head to the University District.

I stepped on a bus headed for the University with the bus pass given to me by the mental health center. I sat down in the first open seat I could find. There weren't many, and I peered around. The people had places to go, had paychecks to earn, and degrees on their walls. I wanted to be one of them. I felt like an imposter as if I didn't belong on the same bus. I should be back at the Leopard building, in a box, waiting to receive my next disability check, avoiding the emergency room, occupying the shadows of society like a rat.

There were transportation security guards prowling the bus, looking for criminals to eject. My whiteness provided cover, but I still felt like I didn't belong. Everyone on the bus was busy working on their phones or tablets. I didn't have an electronic device to stare at, so my gaze wandered, scanning the other passengers, making them uncomfortable. I was not able to blend in. My awkward glare caught the eye of a young, blonde woman, professionally dressed in a blouse that accentuated her hourglass frame. She was a beautiful woman, full-figured, sitting directly across from me, legs crossed, in a center facing seat. She nodded her head sideways as if to non-verbally inquire what outcome my eye contact was intended for. Of course, it was meaningless. I had no intentions at all, just captivated by her for a second. But she held eye contact with a strong presence.

"Can I help you?" she asked. "Do you need something?"

"Oh, um. No. I don't know. Sorry," I responded. Obviously flustered with anxiety.

"It's okay," she said. "No worries."

Her attention returned to her device. Later in the day, she wouldn't even recall my existence. I wanted to ask her something. I couldn't think of anything. I was frozen with fear. If I had been interacting with a female in the Jungle a few months earlier, I would have reacted with a direct response, purposed at making money for Rita, with the security of the twins in my shadow. But in this setting, I was a foreigner.

The metro bus emerged from the tunnel, and natural light-filled the interior of the vessel as it slowed to a stop. Passengers arose to their feet in unison. I followed the sheep and my eyes followed the blonde as she turned toward the front of the bus. She stepped directly in front of me like the last train leaving a destitute station. My eyes involuntarily stared at her caboose as it moved gracefully away. A deep breath filled my lungs as I realized I had zero chance to cavort with such a female in this world. At least in my current status as a substance-addicted mental patient.

I followed the sheep out of the bus tunnel, walked up the steps and found myself on the margins of the University of Washington campus once again. I was on the north side of campus, opposite from the Arboretum, and I wisely decided to avoid the Ave where I may have run into former associates.

I was there to dip my toe back into the square culture. I was relatively stable on my medication, and the voices were not bothering me. The combination of meds I was on were not fogging my mind either. So, I felt somewhat lucid. I wondered what would happen if I walked into the admissions office and asked to re-enroll. If I would even be able to keep the credits, I had earned over my first year of college. I walked curiously along the sidewalk near the bus station. The admissions office wasn't far. I was standing in front of it a few minutes later.

The admissions building is an ugly bunker-like concrete structure. It looks like a giant child put it together, stacking rectangular blocks on top of each other to form the floors. I stood there for several minutes, staring at the building. My mental status was organized enough to think through my actions before walking into the building and blindly announcing my presence to the University, which could trigger a phone call to my parents. I didn't want to blow my cover, although I was growing more open to it. I am mentally stable, physically stable, living in the Leopard building with a key in my pocket. I wasn't running from voices and trying to survive anymore. Thoughts rushed through my mind about my journey. I'd navigated psychosis over the previous months. I'd been privileged with sensational acquaintances, and somehow, I was standing at the doorstep of my previous life with an added level of industriousness.

My homelessness was over, and I had a chance to reflect. The wild ride I had been on since the onset of my schizophrenia, since I started hearing the voices, had straightened out. Re-enrolling in school was the most ideal way to re-introduce myself to the square world that I could think of. At least my parents would see that I haven't given up on my previous life, and I want to continue my education. It seemed like the safest way to pop back onto the radar.

However, I decided not to act on my impulse to walk into the admissions office on that day. I wanted to give it more consideration. I hopped back on the bus and went back to the Leopard to consider my options. As I approached my apartment door, I noticed that Desire's door was ajar, and I could hear her rattling around like a packrat. So, I pushed the door open to see a new half-gallon of Black Velvet sitting on her counter, staring at me like a seductive vixen, begging me to wet my whistle.

"Oh hey, sweetheart. How are you today?" Desiree emerged from the bathroom to see me staring at her booze.

"Go ahead. I can see you wanna grab a drink. You look like you've just seen a ghost or something."

"I'm thinking about going back to my old life. I may leave here soon."

"Old life, huh? You gonna sell your ass again?" Desiree was a world-class ball-buster. "I'm just kiddin, sweetheart. Are you thinkin about going home to your parents then? I think you should. If I had someone out there who loved me and wanted to take care of me, I'd go too."

Desiree made a good point regarding the love I was choosing not to accept from my parents.

"Kind of. I may just enroll back into college. If I do that, the admissions office will call my folks and let them know. I guess that would be going back to my parents."

"Enroll back in college?" Desiree cackled. "So, you don't have to be here at all?"

"Nope."

"Well, lots of people get kicked out of their families for being crazy, but it sounds like you just quit your family. You didn't get kicked out. You chose to leave and become a bum. Is that right?"

"That's correct," Desiree was making a pretty clear point, and I was feeling like a piece of shit.

244

"Now, I'm not trying to make you feel too bad here," she said, "but you do have some options. Were you in school when the voices started talking in your head?" Desiree asked.

"Yup. Actually, I was sitting in a big class when it happened. I stood up and started talking to them in front of everyone in the middle of a lecture. I was yelping and hollering. Then security came and took me off to the University jail until my parents showed up. It's pretty funny thinking back now." We enjoyed a good laugh for a second before being interrupted by a loud knock at the door, which startled both of us.

"I don't know who that could be. Nobody knows I'm even here or gives a fuck," Desiree said. I walked up to her door and peered through the peephole, but nobody was there.

"I don't see anyone out there," I said as I opened the door a crack to see two well-groomed professionals standing in front of my apartment next door, a man and a woman. They knocked so loud Desiree, and I thought they were knocking on her door. They clearly didn't care who knew they were there.

"Do you know who lives here?!" The man shouted as he saw me peering out of Desiree's apartment like a scared child. I opened the door wider and stepped under the door frame.

"No, I don't know him. He just moved in. I haven't even seen him yet. I just heard him a little bit last night." I lied.

"Well, we have some questions for him," the female stated with authority over the man. She approached, so I stepped into the hallway and closed the door to make sure they didn't see Desiree in her apartment, as if they would know who the actual tenant was. She handed me a business card: Dina Blood, Seattle Police Department Homicide Detective. I felt a brick dropping from my throat to my stomach.

"Okay," my voice quivered with anxiety. "I'll give him this card."

"Thanks. Feel free to call me when you know he's home," the Detective said with persuasive charisma. She smiled and made me feel comfortable as she held eye contact for several seconds. Then she walked away and waved for the male detective to follow.

I twisted the door handle and stepped back into Desiree's apartment as if it were my own, shaking with nerves. I assumed they were looking for me connected to Tex's murder back in the Jungle. Why else?

"Well, shit, sweetheart. Maybe you're not that sweet after all. Those murder police have got you rattled like hell. Plus, you just lied to them. Not that you need to, but feel free to share, my dear." Not much got passed, Desiree. She poured a few ounces of Black Velvet into my plastic cup and looked me in the eye, deep into my soul.

"Okay. Well, I was camping out in the Jungle a while back with a group of drug runners. A couple of members of the group beat this guy to death in front of a bunch of Jungle campers. I was there, and I was involved. But the guy had it coming. He deserved to die.

"Hold on. I was there for that. You mean when Rita's boys stomped that guy to death?"

"Ah, yeah, do you know Rita?" I said with disbelief. Was Desiree in the Jungle at the same time?

"Haha, know her? Not really. But I've been around the Jungle for years and years. Have I met her? Yes. Would she remember me? No, probably not. She's not someone I would fuck with at all. But we did hook up a couple of times years ago. Probably 15 years ago. At the time, she was shacked up with some biker, but he let her fuck around with other women. Or maybe he didn't have a choice. She ordered him around. How did you hook up with Rita?"

"It was right after I got out of jail, and I followed a couple of guys to the Jungle looking for a place to sleep. She basically took me in. She said her son had schizophrenia, so she wanted to help me because I reminded her of him."

"Shit. Well, I don't know much about her other than she loved jamming my face into her crotch for a couple of nights.

But I also know that she's no joke. This wasn't the first guy she'd killed. She's long gone. Tons of people know who Rita is, and they know she ordered those two big black boys to beat that dude to death. What did the guy do to get himself murdered anyway?"

"He was basically preying on homeless kids, getting them addicted to heroin and then raping them when they were all fucked up."

"Well, a lot of Jungle folks witnessed that beating. Somebody living here now may have seen it up close and then recognized you when you moved in here. That could be why the murder police are knocking on your door," Desiree stated the obvious. "Maybe this would be a good time for you to go back to your old self. To sink back into a life where nobody will recognize you from the Jungle."

I realized it was likely I would never step foot back into my apartment at the Leopard Building.

"Can I trust you?" I asked Desiree who would hold my fate in her hands when the cops came back looking for me. After they figured out that they were talking to me, could I even return to school as a University student in this town?

"Can you trust me? Have another drink before you go back on the lamb, son. You can sleep here tonight if you want. But I'm not gonna deny it to the cops. I'm not gonna confirm either. I don't know anything, just some lonely-drunk-neighbor who desperately lured you into a conversation with booze."

"Wow. Thanks, Desiree."

"Shut up and drink, dammit. But you have to tell me, what was Rita like with you?"

"I think she wanted to help me because of her son. She felt like she failed him and could somehow atone for that by fixing me. I don't think I'm the first whack-job she's tried to talk out of being crazy, either. She's always got a project going on. She's a social worker at heart. In real life, she's a violent drug runner with a vicious crew of killers who would die for her."

"So, let me get it straight then, you were adopted into Rita's crew cause you caught the crazy voices? Which made her into a mother-type figure or some shit?"

"I mean. It's obviously complicated," I said with my palms up.

"Is she still into ladies? Or does she have a man?"

"She likes the ladies, no doubt. She wasn't fucking around much when I was with the Ranch Crew."

"Ranch crew? Is that what y'all called yourselves? That's cute." Ballbusting.

So, I went on to discuss my time on the Ranch with Desiree. She got a real kick out of it. We stayed up most of the night bullshitting. It got my mind off of the cops who were looking for me. I woke up in the same Adirondack chair I had been sitting in the next morning, and Desiree didn't want me to stay much longer.

"I said you could stay the night. One night. So you gotta decide, sweetheart. Are you gonna go back to college like a good boy, or go back to your apartment next door? Stick around. That's what I want. I can give you whiskey and be your mommy. Just like Rita."

"You just ask for it, Desiree. I'm bout to smack you down the hall," I was comfortable busting Desiree's large balls at this point.

"Oh, I found my next abuser! Just get your shit together and get out, sweetheart. You ain't nobody's abuser. I need a lot more than that. Just grease your vagina and move on."

"Don't fuck me over, Desiree. I have a life to live."

"You sure do. Such a nice little life. Leaving all these bums in your wake. But I don't blame you." Desiree reminded me of my immense privilege. Nobody else in the building had any other option than to be there. I was dripping with guilt.

I struggled to wedge a shitty pair of shoes on my dirty feet with no socks. Leaning back in Desree's Adirondack chair. I looked her in the eyes without saying a word and swung my torso forward, rocking to my feet. I turned my back and twisted the doorknob stepping into the hallway, closing the door behind me. I was still crazy without the pills. I needed my psych meds. So, I stepped back into my apartment, which I had planned not to do, and grabbed the medication set I left.

Chapter 23

As I attempted to sprint through the lobby, I was accosted by a member of the Leopard Building front desk staff.

"Jack, is that you?" An anxious Leopard building staff member asked. "We have someone we need you to talk to. Let me call her."

I walked past her as if I didn't hear what she said. She gave the good old college effort. Perhaps I would sit next to her in class later in the school year, I thought. I was out the door, never to return. I was on a path to redemption as I stepped back onto the sidewalk I'd become very familiar with over the past few days. I could smell the humanity, urine dripping off the sidewalk. Turning my back toward the street, I looked up at the Leopard Building in all its glory. She was once an upscale motel. Moving on.

I felt confident as I rode the bus to the University District. I had a purpose. I was going to get my life back, with the assistance of psychotropic medication, of course. I looked around the bus on the way up to the U District, hoping for eye contact. I wanted to tell someone what I was about to do: walk into that admissions office and announce my return.

Stepping out of the bus with a puffed chest, I desired for direct human interaction. I wanted to speak with anyone about anything. I was ready to tell the story about mental illness like a faithful martyr. This was a liberal enough campus to glorify my schizophrenic escapades. I just needed to find the right audience—a sympathetic perspective. Perhaps a harem of beautiful bleeding-heart coeds would be interested. I could be a guest speaker on the Psych 101 tour.

I floated over the sidewalk as I approached the homeless kids on the Ave. There were four adolescents passed out on the sidewalk. I could see an outreach worker circling, looking for a subject for Narcan. She sniffed around the sidewalk like a vulture. However, her purpose was to save lives, not feed off the dead. She was a rare breed: human with altruism. She only wanted to help them live. But they were under the control of another version of Tex shepherding his sheep. This damaged sociopath must have been tortured at a very young age to feel compelled to manipulate the most vulnerable people he could find. I just walked past and made my way toward the admissions building.

I shuffled up the concrete steps and approached the lobby of the admissions office as a much different person than the one who last attended classes at the University of Washington. I stepped up to the receptionist, who locked her eyes onto mine assertively. Prospective students in the lobby stared at me with curiosity. I was clearly lost, not in the right place, like a monkey walking outside of his cage at the zoo, pretending to be a human.

"Can I help you?" asked the middle-aged Caucasian receptionist.

"I don't know," I responded as I stumbled over my words, laboring to collect my thoughts.

"Well, why are you here?" The receptionist quipped with a cutting tone. Miffed, I sharpened my tone and the words spewed from my breath with the force of a firehose. Suddenly the forceful assertiveness I had learned from my time in the jungle took over:

"Hey! I'm here to get help! I was a student here, and I got lost. I'm here to find my way back. That's why I'm here!" Perhaps I was intentionally vague.

"Sir, you need to lower your voice, or security will escort you out."

"I have a mental breakdown and try to get help, and this is how you react? Forcefully throw me out? Go ahead and call them. Do what you gotta do! If this is how you want to treat your students who go crazy, then just do it!" I extended liberty by referring to myself as a student, but it hadn't been *that* long.

It worked. Screaming angrily attracted enough attention to expose myself. Administrators began pouring into the lobby, surrounding me with a show of force, which was appropriate as I presented a pretty clear threat. I peered around at them and shouted:

254

"Remember me? I'm the guy who went crazy in class. Has anyone been looking for me?"

Suddenly I could see the realization come over a couple of faces in the room. They knew who I was.

"Jack?" one of them asked.

"Yes! There you go." I pointed at the neatly dressed woman who identified me. "That's me. I'm back after a long, twisted journey, and I'd like for someone to contact my parents."

"Jack, my name is Karen. I'm the director of admissions. Why don't you come back to my office with me, and we'll make that call to your parents and also see what else we can do for you?"

I thanked the receptionist sardonically and informed the rest of the people in the lobby that, "The show is over." Karen marched me back to her office confidently and plopped me in front of her desk.

"Jack, state for me your date of birth and last name so I can confirm your identity," Karen instructed me as her assistant handed me a bottle of water. I complied, provided my square identity, my original paper identity. Karen pecked away at her keyboard for a couple of minutes before peering back over at me.

"Yep, that's you, Jack," she said, rotating her computer screen into my view so I could see a campus alert that was issued around the time I went missing. It had a large picture of my face. I recognized the photo. It was from my student ID card. I then turned my head toward the shiny, reflective glass window in Karen's office to see a vague, disheveled reflection of my current appearance as my two identities were crossing paths like pirate ships in the night. Ignoring each other for self-preservation's sake. Karen punched the speakerphone button on her office phone and announced:

"I'm dialing your parent's home number. My assistant is also calling an ambulance to take you to the University Hospital for evaluation."

Karen wasn't asking for my permission. The phone rang only once before my mother's voice bounced off the walls, filling the room with a familiar, pleasant sound.

"Hello, Ma'am, this is Karen Attler from the University of Washington admissions office. I'm sorry to call you so abruptly, but I have some urgent information for you."

"Okay..." My Mother responded with pessimistic curiosity.

"Your son Jack is sitting here in my office. He just presented here this morning and requested that we contact you. " The room filled with silence.

"Hey, Mom," I said to interrupt the awkwardness.

"Jack, is that really you?"

"It is. Or some version of me at least."

256

The sound of my mother sobbing dripped out of the phone as if the receiver was producing tears itself.

Karen interrupted: "I've had my staff arrange medical transport for Jack. We are sending him to the University Medical Center for evaluation by medical and mental health professionals. You should make arrangements to see him soon, if possible."

Suddenly the call was over, and Karen was escorting me back to the lobby, where medics were waiting to strap me onto a stretcher and roll me off to get fixed up. I began to worry that they would draw my blood and see that I have antipsychotic medication in my system and somehow expose my alternate identity. But, I was past the point of no return. Plus, I could just tell them I got the meds from another homeless guy. Whatever. I could probably tell them anything because they will have no idea what I've been doing, where I've been. No idea about Rita or the Leopard building, none of it. How could they?

I submitted to the medics, who buckled me onto the stretcher, and rolled me out of the building and into an ambulance parked on the sidewalk. It was a short ride, about three blocks to the University Hospital. Suddenly I was being processed into the emergency department. Initially, I declined to answer any open-ended questions and just requested meal service. Within four hours, my parents were

257

at my bedside, draped all over me. I'd forgotten how much I loved them. I couldn't stop apologizing for what I'd put them through.

"I'm so sorry, Mom," I stated tearfully.

"Oh honey, we're just so happy to see you alive. Nothing else matters."

"Mom, I want to get better. I want to go back to school and continue on that path."

"Son," my Dad jumped into the conversation, his voice trembling with emotion, "we want to take you home to Wenatchee with us and work with some local shrinks, really commit to getting you stable. Then we can work on getting you back into school, your old life, whatever you want. But you have an issue that we need to manage, and no therapist will talk you out of it. You need to take some medication to deal with this, my boy."

"I know, Dad. I've actually been taking meds I got from another crazy guy on the street, and they actually work," I issued a necessary lie to protect my alternate identity.

"Okay, well, I'm glad to hear that, son. I guess maybe you learned that lesson the hard way," my father stated ominously. I thought that was an insightful thing for my father to say. I certainly hadn't taken an easy route to navigating through my illness. But, does anyone really learn how to deal with schizophrenia easily? Does anyone learn

258

how to cope with these symptoms quickly and maintain a high level of functioning? Does anyone really have the answer? If so, does it apply generally? As I pondered the meaning of life, I had a number of shrinks buzzing around me who I could have consulted with—psychiatrists who may have a well-developed, research based answer to my questions. But I didn't want to listen to them.

"Totally. Dad, let's get out of here. I don't need to see anyone. I'm ready to get in the car and go straight to whichever shrink you'd like me to see in the Wenatchee valley. Seriously, I think it's best if you get me out of this environment."

Chapter 24

I sat there in my hospital bed waiting for my father to respond when a familiar face poked his head into the doorway with a big bright smile. It was Alvin, the charming drug dealer I met in jail. But he was dressed like a square, clean cut.

"Knock knock. How you doin Jack?"

"Alvin? What are *you* doing here?"

"Well, Jack, that's where it gets complicated." He shifted his jacket away from his belt line to expose a police badge. "Sir, do you mind if I have a quick word in private with Jack?"

My father looked stupefied, "What's this all about?" His voice was full of fear, and I could feel how much he loved me.

"Look, sir, it won't take long. I just have a couple of questions for Jack."

My parents exited the room, and Alvin shut the door behind him. I was frozen with confusion. Alvin sat down in the chair next to the bed. I was sitting up at attention.

"What? You're a cop! What kind of cop tries to find junkies to sell drugs to in a county jail?" My Jungle assertiveness was kicking in again.

"The undercover kind. I was looking for informants. I'm a detective in the Vice unit, so my job is to gather information about who is running drugs on the street. Which is why I was so surprised when I learned you had hooked in with Rita's crew in the Jungle."

"I don't know what you are talking about," my instinct was to protect the crew, especially Rita."

"It's okay, Jack. I'm not interested in you at all. Don't worry about that," Alvin said as he stood up and walked over to the door, opened it and gestured someone in from the hallway. In walked Rita.

"How ya doin Jackie?"

"Wait," I got up out of the bed, "let me get this straight: Alvin is a drug cop?"

"Correct," they both confirmed simultaneously.

"So why are we all here?"

"That's what I'm trying to get to Jack," Alvin moved in to explain.

"Just hold on a second there, Alvin," Rita interrupted and took control of the conversation, "Yes, Alvin is a drug cop. And *we* were running drugs, quite a bit of drugs. But the way it works with these drug cops is that they're always looking for a bigger fish to fry. Which I provided to him, someone way above me, and I'm not even talking about the Gypsy

Jokers either, Jack. I've given them one of the cartel bosses. This guy controls the entire Pacific Northwest."

"Okay, great. So what do you need from me, Rita?"

"Well, Jackie, I don't need anything from you. But I owe you some money. You were a contributing member of the Ranch crew, and I need to make you whole. I've come here today to give you your cut from the operation. But, in order for me to get such a favorable deal from Alvin here, sweetheart that he is, I had to cut him into the Ranch payout. So, we have sliced up the pie one more time. Anyway, the other members of the crew each earned about 90 thousand bucks, give or take. Because you were sort of a trainee, I had you budgeted for a smaller percentage, for about 50 thousand. But because we are doing business with a dirty cop, I had to cut that in half."

Rita reached her hand into a coat pocket and pulled out two big envelopes, handing one of them to each of us.

"It is nice doing business with you, Rita. I know I'll never see you again, so good luck in the witness protection program," Alvin said smugly.

"Thanks, Alvin. That's right, Jack, this will be our last visit. Alvin pulled a couple of strings for me. Otherwise, the cartel would find me easily and kill me. I actually need to get moving quickly and hide under a rock for the rest of my days. I know you will keep your mouth shut about where that

262

money came from. It would be very dangerous if you didn't. That goes for both of you."

"Of course, Rita."

The two of them stood up, walked to the door and left. I crawled back into the bed and tucked the envelope of money under the cover with me before my parents came back in from the hallway.

"What was that, Jack," my mother asked with a somber tone.

"Oh nothing, Mom. Just a cop who wanted to confirm my identity. I was a missing person for quite a while." My parents seemed to buy that explanation. I could feel the envelope sitting against my leg. Suddenly I wasn't so sure about going back to Wenatchee with my parents. I imagined some of the things I could do with that $25,000.

My Dad started back into the conversation we were having before Rita and Alvin showed up: "Listen, Jack, if you are ready to go home, I think we can just go ahead and leave. I'll go talk with the medical staff here and see what they need from us.

"That sounds good, Dad," I said as I shifted my weight around in the bed, allowing me to tuck the envelope into my underwear. "Why don't you both go talk with the medical staff. I'll wait here and rest."

"Okay, son, we'll be back shortly."

When they returned, I was gone again.

END